I0607533

SANITY CLAUSE IS COMING...

A SECOND ANTHOLOGY OF TWISTED CHRISTMAS TALES

Edited By Theresa Derwin

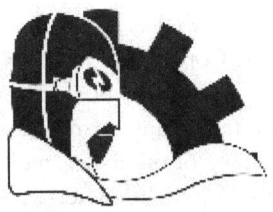

www.fringeworks.co.uk

EDITED BY THERESA DERWIN
COVER BY DARELL BEVAN

'Foreword' © Theresa Derwin
'I Saw Mommy Killing Santa Claus' © Roger Clark
'The Curious Case of the Cake Maker and his Christmas Zombies' © Sean T Page
'The Emissary Goat' © Colin Fisher
'Satan Vs Santa' © Colleen Chen
'All Holiday Special with Magritte' © Brandon Cracraft
'The Furst Noel' © Edward Beat
'A Visit from Santa' © Dave Williamson
'Prancer's Story' © U Z Eliserio
'The Without Man' © L. F. Robertson
'Christmas Glitch' © Carl Lambein Jr
'The Egg Man' © Fiona Moore
'Killer Reindeer' © Spencer Carvalho
'Pantocrime' © Andrew Lawston

Copyright © 2014, Fringeworks Ltd

Cover art: Darrel Bevan, with colorisation by Anna Higgins

ISBN: 978-1-909573-14-7

Published 2014
Fringeworks Ltd, Y Berllan, Maen Y Groes, Cei Newydd, Ceredigion, SA45 9TR.

DEDICATION

This is dedicated to Joel Lane (1963–2013). I am privileged to have published Joel's story 'Winter Song' in *Ain't No Sanity Clause* in 2012. I am more privileged to have actually known Joel. He was a talented writer, a true gentleman and an inspiration to us all. He valiantly fought the corner of those less fortunate than himself and deservedly won the World Fantasy Award for *Where Furnaces Burn* (PS Publishing) just three weeks before he passed away. He will be sadly missed by all who knew him.

CONTENTS

FOREWORD
by Theresa Derwin

It's that time of year again; lights are twinkling in the street, the trees are appearing in the odd window and all of the shops have their Christmas displays up. And you know what? I love it. Despite the money I'll have to spend, despite the fact I'll probably gain half a stone and be pig sick of turkey I still love it. So what does Christmas mean to me?

Let's be honest here, I love the presents. Who doesn't? This year off my Dad I have Honeymania shower gel and perfume, two Christmas romance books (I'm a sucker for those) and a reindeer hoodie onesie (yes, sexy I know!) from me to me, a big box of Hotel Chocolat chocolates. And I know I'll get some lovely surprises from friends and family. But I love giving the presents too. I love finding that right thing that makes someone smile because they're delighted and because they know you're thinking of them. That special present. For Dad, who's a bloke and therefore inherently difficult, it's a jumper and whiskey and for my sis Tish, smellies galore. And that elusive bottle of perfume that I seem to have, er, lost! But suffice to say apart from the fact I've her main present is in my wardrobe somewhere, I know her enough to know she'll be happy. But I also bought her an early present, a book about two sisters who often have sibling rivalry, and don't always understand each other so swap Christmasses to see how the other show fits. I can't exactly do that with my sis, no way would I be able to teach the little kids she teaches, but I at least wrapped up some of her Christmas presents for her family and friends to alleviate some of the stress that inevitably comes with the season. And that brings me in a round about way to the main reason I love Christmas. Spending time with my family and friends.

Last year my sis, brother in law and niece and nephew were at a wedding so it was just me. Dad and Uncle John, but this year it's back to the normal madness of our family life. I'll give you an idea of what that's like. A few years ago my sis bought the two boys (nephew now 23 and brother-in-law 49) a giant inflatable hamster wheel, so we spent the day drinking, eating and rolling down the stairs and round the living room like nutters. Great fun. And after we open the presents together and ooh and aah we eat with dodgy paper hats and dodgier jokes, but it's all part of the fun. And for just a while my very stressed and busy sister smiles and laughs and the stress disappears.

But with it comes the inevitable sadness. On the cabinet by the dining table at my sisters house is a photo of my Auntie Loylie from a Christmas a few years ago. She has this amazing red hair and is looking grinning at the camera with a pink feather boa round her neck and she looks just like a mischievous elf. And I miss her

deeply at that point. I remember other Christmases with her and wish there'd been more. Every year my sis goes to the grave, and we visit Moms grave too. I was three when Mom passed away so the pain of losing Loylie and missing her at Christmas is deeper, closer, but the emptiness and wishing I could remember one Christmas with Mom is buried deep inside. And I feel for my sis because she knew Mom. It must be a deeper loss for her. Then there's uncle Johnny with a huge beaming smile and broad Irish accent, who was fervently religious and made me feel a bit of a heathen for only going to church at weddings, funerals and Christmas Eve with the family. I miss Johnny too. I miss them all, the many who have passed away. And I feel for those who have lost someone recently and this will be there first Christmas without their *someone special*. If you've read the dedication, you'll see we have lost a dear friend and talented writer, Joel Lane. I feel for Joel's friends and family, for the writing community and his Mom in particular. Joel was a special, special man and a true talent. And would not want to see us weeping, despite the bleak nature of his horror! So I'm thinking of you out there - those who are left.

I wish I could see every single one of my family and friends this Christmas but it isn't always possible, be it my health or theirs, or the distance, but it doesn't mean I love them any less. I think about those family members and friends at this time of year and wonder how many more Christmases I will still have them. Which is why Dad and I sit and write over a hundred Christmas cards and send them to Ireland, Australia and across the UK. We write them and send them to say 'we love you and are thinking of you'. And this is why, much to the amusement of my family and friends, I watch silly Christmas films, colour in my colouring books, read Christmas horror and eat gingerbread until I explode. So I can celebrate Christmas my way and forget the pain of those who have gone, remember them with love, phone and write to those who are left, revel in the madness that is Christmas and spend time with the most important people in the world; my friends and my wonderful, bat shit crazy family.

So please have a Merry Christmas this year, raise a toast to those who are gone, but show your love to those who are left behind. And immerse yourself into a world of Christmas horror and fantasy. I hope you enjoy this book as much as I enjoyed editing it.

Theresa Derwin

I SAW MOMMY KILLING SANTA CLAUS
by Roger Clark

Martin stood in the crisp, cold winter's night, silently looking up at the gothic architecture of the old department store.

After his actions earlier in the day, he wondered why he'd been invited back, but Santa, the Elves and the workers in the toy department were so insistent that he return and so he left as if he had no choice. Probably something perverted going on, he thought. Who would invite a fourteen year old boy back to a kid's grotto after midnight?

Of course, everyone from 'Lost Property' had forbidden him to go and had grounded him. 'Lost Property' was what he and the others had named the home. The orphanage didn't like that image and so it suited him just fine to make sure he used the name.

He could understand why he had been forbidden to come back to the shop and the grotto. Firstly, he'd made sure that everyone had known of his displeasure at having to go in the first place. Martin didn't like Christmas.

He'd complained as much as possible. He'd refused breakfast, was deliberately late to the mini-bus and had misbehaved as much as he could to get out of the trip. Besides hating Christmas, why would a teenager want to go and see Father Christmas anyway?

The trip had been organised for months and had been sponsored by the department store. Every year, they contributed financially to the setting up of the grotto in their store by a company specialising in them across the country; probably the world.

It was one of Martin's ideas of what hell must be like. To be stuck in a job thinking of Christmas all the while, organising the disappointment of millions who just would not get what they wanted year on year.

As his misty breath formed a variety of shapes in the air, he pulled his rucksack closer and could feel the weight of the contents. He'd got every aerosol he could find, lots of paper, lighter fuel, matches and candles. His biggest find was the small container of petrol from the back yard that was used for the generator or maybe as an emergency supply for the minibus. They should have hidden it better. Probably laws about that sort of thing.

He was only a skinny and thin fourteen year old. Pale in complexion, he always surprised people with his strength. He had earlier, when he'd run amok in the grotto and he was determined to now. That's why he'd returned; to show these people that they couldn't go on making false promises.

Christmas was fake. Everything about it was fake and he hated it. He had grown up believing in Santa, waiting for him to bring him the latest toy or his favourite treats to eat but, no, not once. Santa let him down, year after year.

Christmas was always miserable. For some reason it was always a time when relatives died or had arguments. It seemed like every year they lost someone dear to them until there was really only him and his parents. Even his long line of pets seemed to be poisoned, get run over or something just before the big day.

Despite everything said in the school playground, he'd held on to his belief in Santa. Perhaps for too long and he didn't know why. Not once had he delivered what he wanted.

As he'd grown older, he'd asked Santa for no one to die; for Dad to stop drinking; for his parents to get jobs; for them to stop fighting.

The fighting had always got worse nearer to Christmas. He usually hid in his room or pretended not to notice. Over the years, he'd got braver until he started telling them to stop. That just made them focus their attention on him and he'd got hurt more than once.

Santa would stop it wouldn't he? He had never done anything before so perhaps one year, he hoped, Santa would pull off a Christmas miracle.

When he was ten, on Christmas Eve, he had heard his parents arguing again in the middle of the night. It had gone quiet for quite some time until he heard some rustling and things being dragged down the stairs.

Hoping to see Santa delivering the presents, he slowly opened his door and crept downstairs. There he saw his drunken Dad with the presents, laying them out. His mother had been crying again and was trying to put a few more presents out.

Martin couldn't remember much more than that. He'd seen the fight start but couldn't remember what it was over. Next thing he remembered was seeing the Christmas tree tumble in slow motion; the knife and the blood.

One parent dead. One in prison. Martin put in a home. Another reason to love Christmas.

He looked at his watch. Gone midnight; that was the time they'd said to go in but there was no one around.

The lights of the store were always on of a night and he'd noticed that there were no security shutters down over the windows and doors. There weren't even any blinking lights on the security cameras. They were just asking for trouble here and he was going to give it to them.

The other kids in the home had started to nickname him 'Scrooge' or 'Grinch' because of his dislike of everything Christmas. He didn't like any of them anyway and had come to delight in ruining anything to do with the season for as many people as possible.

This would be his crowning glory; setting fire to Santa's Grotto. He smiled to himself as he walked over to the door to peer inside. He leaned on the door to take a look through the glass and it moved. It moved. It was open.

Martin couldn't believe it. What idiots would leave the doors open to a department store overnight without any security?

He checked the old-fashioned security cameras again and noted that the lights were still not blinking. The door opened easily as he pushed on it and no alarms sounded. This was going to be *too* easy.

Just in case there was anyone watching, Martin decided to make his way to the grotto first. If no one was there he would get it ready to burn. The whole lot should go up a treat. He'd douse it with petrol, set everything up ready to light and then go and do some free shopping before starting the fire.

There was no doubt that an empty department store in the middle of the night was creepy though. He could see no one around as he walked through the aromas that were still hanging in the air of the perfume department.

The escalators were making their rhythmic sounds; chugging away monotonously about their business, inviting him to the next floor where the grotto was.

He walked up instead of just standing there, anxious to get started and see why he'd been invited. He was more of the opinion now that the whole things was a stupid scam or that they hadn't expected him to come. At least they'd dropped the charges.

As he got to the top of the stairs, something small and green had caught his eye. It was fast and had run past the bottom of the escalators, making him jump. Just as he got off the top of the stairs, he was sure he saw the same thing run past a coat rack that had been placed in just the right spot to catch the eye of the mothers bringing their kids to the grotto. *That would have to go*, he thought.

He crouched down and peered over at the coats. There was something under there; something green; bright green with some sort of white fur. He put his rucksack down and crept forward. No one was going to make a fool out of him.

As he reached the coat rack, whatever it was jumped out at him. The coats went flying over the shop floor as the thing jumped on his chest and fled. Martin was sure he'd heard a child-like laugh as it did so and another sound. Yes, that was it!

He'd heard a small bell and quickly put the facts together. It was one of those stupid Elves they had employed at the Grotto. He'd never seen anything like them before this year except in books or on TV but one of them had just jumped him.

He grabbed his rucksack and set off for the grotto. It didn't matter that there were people here now; in fact it would be even better. It would be funny to see those little Elves running from burning tinsel.

The rest of the shop floor was in darkness that made the entrance to the grotto even more 'Christmassy'. The neat wooden fence around the fake snow stood at hip height and lights had been woven in and out of the wood.

This reflected on the snow and the two snowmen that proudly stood either side of the entrance to a tacky igloo affair. The entrance to the igloo was longer than normal and formed a dark corridor for visitors to walk down and see a variety of Christmas scenes.

Martin made his way to the little wooden gate and was startled as Christmas music started to loudly blast from inside the grotto. The Elves ran past again and he was sure that the snowmen hadn't had bright red eyes earlier in the day.

As he walked the small path to the Igloo, he heard the high pitched sound of polystyrene rubbing against each other and caught the heads of the snowmen following him; watching with their deep red eyes.

He was being stupid. They must be animatronics or something. He walked straight passed and into the Igloo.

This was not how it was earlier in the day. As the music slowed so that it sounded really off-pitch, Martin quickened his step past the half-eaten gingerbread men, the melting snowmen and the reindeer which were missing their antlers and had bloodied stumps instead.

He didn't know whether to laugh or to just double back and get the hell out of there. However, he was not going to be made a fool of by anyone and was now more determined than ever to set the fire no matter what the consequences.

Martin reached the main waiting area. A dark room with glow-in-the-dark snow painted on the black walls where the queue to see Santa grew all day long. A deep, echoing voice boomed from the next room that sent a chill through to his bones. All it said was one word over and over.

'Ho Ho Ho'.

Whoever was making that noise, (either properly or through some sort of special sound effect), was certainly not getting it right. It was more to do with a horror movie than Christmas.

It echoed through the room again and only stirred Martin on further. He went into the next room which, again, was now different from what he'd seen earlier in the day. Instead of the tinsel and festive 'delights' there was just one large Christmas tree and Santa's chair. The exit door had also seemed to disappear.

The tree was huge. Martin struggled to see the top of it and the sides reached out impossibly into what was really a huge hall and not a room at all. It suddenly struck him how tall it was; too tall to fit in the shop. And then there was the colour of it...

A light shone brightly somewhere above indicating a star on top. This highlighted the deep, ash coloured branches covered in space-black thorns and tinsel. Every branch had a red ribbon tied neatly in a bow holding up a glass bauble with a grey mist streaking about inside like some old London fog.

Santa was sitting on the chair.

He hadn't been there before and Martin hadn't seen where he'd come from.

'What the hell is all this man?'

Martin moved forward to stand in front of Santa, surprised that his voice hadn't wavered.

'Ho. Ho. Ho.' It was the same voice as earlier. 'Thank you for taking up my invitation young Martin.'

Santa stood and Martin noticed his beard peeling away, his costume stained with soot. But it was those eyes that made Martin step back. They were black; deep, deep, black. Sucking in light like a black hole, they were so dark that Martin couldn't see the creatures' eye-lids.

Martin had stopped referring to it as Santa but as 'the creature' and this was proven as it reached down from its great height and held him by the shoulders. Martin took in a sharp breath as the bony hands dug into his skin.

'What do you want? What are you?'

'The same questions as always.' The voice was becoming less deep and more of a loud whisper.

This was when the Elves from earlier came in to the room. Small and squat with large bulbous heads, their eyes stared at Martin for a while before they looked at each other, held their stomachs and let out a huge child-like laugh. This showed row upon row of razor-sharp teeth through their white beards.

As they laughed, they grabbed Santa's cloak and pulled. It came away from the figure easily, covering the grotesque creatures that pulled themselves comically from underneath. However, Martin wasn't watching this.

He was struggling to get away from the creature now holding him. It seemed insubstantial as he kicked its wispy body. Black tendrils of smoke whipped around as the beard fell off and pulled the rest of the face with it, revealing an elongated black skeletal head. In various shades of black and grey, it seemed to be a monstrous cross between Santa and an angel.

Fingers holding on to Martin elongated and the wisps of smoke wound their way into his ears while others forced themselves down his screaming throat and covered his eyes.

Above his attempted screams, and the laughter of the Elves, the creature whispered its final words to Martin; 'Know me.'

And Martin did. The creature fed Martin details of what it was; a creature created from the very resentment of Christmas; one that nurtured and collected dark souls for its own amusement. Sometimes it helped create the resentment but then there were others who didn't need any help.

As Martin found out how it had manipulated all those Christmas events, he saw his flesh peel and fall to the ground. It rotted and melted away until black fumes twisted their way back up to meet the dust that his bones had now crumbled to.

His grey soul was caught by the creature in a glass sphere and it tied a neat red bow to it before carefully hanging it on the tree. It had another soul for its collection.

The Elves were singing '*Oh Christmas Tree*' and laughing.
The creature sat down and waited for the next one.

THE CURIOUS CASE OF THE CAKE-MAKER AND HIS CHRISTMAS ZOMBIES
by Sean T Page

In a dreary corner of a dreary town in the heart of the industrial north of England stood a small cake shop. It had been on there on Lower Medley Street for more than half a century and had once been the finest purveyor of cakes in the whole county of Yorkshire.

But, things were different now. As the icy December rain fell, the shop's current owner, one Mr Silas Cartwright, slammed the front door and locked up for the night. Flaking paint fell as he leant to test the door. *Who would want to break in anyway?* he thought.

The Christmas season is a big time for cake makers everywhere. Christmas cake, chocolate yuletide logs, mince pies—people stock up for their parties and feasts. However, the Cartwright cake shop had been going downhill ever since the giant CakenBake chain, England's first cake and bake warehouse, opened up less than a mile away. With a dedicated ingredients research team back at CakenBake London headquarters, any original recipe Silas created was copied and mass-produced within days, and at half the cost.

For sure, Silas's cake shop would not last another year, not with this kind of competition. It had been in the family for years and alongside his best new baker award of 1991, stood the many trinkets his father and grandfather had collected on their extravagant culinary tours around the world.

Silas waved to Mrs Siddiqui from the off licence across the road and headed back upstairs to his small flat above the shop and another TV dinner with the classic movies he loved.

Next morning on the 22nd December, just two shopping days before Christmas, Silas opened up his shop at nine o'clock as he did every day. He dusted off the tops, checked the enticing window display and flipped the open sign around on the door. But this wasn't the start of his day. He had been up since five o'clock baking up treats for his customers—highly decorated Christmas cakes, moist banana cakes, delightful batenburgs—ideal for those surprise seasonal visitors. He needed to 'shift some sponge' as they say in the cake making business. These few days had to count or things would look very bleak indeed for his shop in the New Year.

The day had started slowly, tailed off in the middle and staggered home at the end. Silas glanced around his small shop. There were unsold cakes, buns and mince pies everywhere. The only thing he had shifted today was the cherry cake for Mrs Siddiqui's birthday party. He had seen hurrying crowds of Christmas shoppers scurrying by—some even stopped and peered at his classic cake shop window display. But, they all walked on. Whatever he made, CakenBake could cook up in a jiffy and at a discount rate. Their two for the price of one offer on Christmas cakes was really taking its toll on Silas's business.

He looked around his shop once more before going into end of day autopilot. Cash up the till, check the fridge units, and sweep the floor.

However, on this particular night, things were about to change and a key link in this chain of events, was one of the delicious glazed cherries which had fallen to the floor, as Silas wrapped up Mrs Siddiqui's specially ordered fruitcake.

As Silas leaned forward to check the till's meagre takings again, he put his foot squarely on the offending sugar fruit and skidded uncontrollably. The money in his hands went high in the air as he swung his arms in wide loops. Cake boxes flew as he fell backwards. One of his flaying arms caught his bookshelf sending not only his recipes flying but also the antique Chinese porcelain dragon bookend his grandfather had brought back from the Far East.

Now, as every reader knows, strange Chinese porcelain is oft the source of mystery in a story and so it will be in this one. But, this fact did not prevent the gaudy red antique being smashed to pieces on the hard tile floor.

Luckily for Silas, the empty cake boxes had provided an ideal set of crash mats. At least there was some benefit in selling so few he thought. His recipe books were less fortunate. His signed copy of Cake-Tastic by star American heart throb and leading bakeroo Mrs Angina Kendal made a messy landing amongst the date and walnut loaves whilst his first edition of Gateaux Royale by Francois LeRoque, whom many considered to be the greatest cake maker all of all time, fared even worse, devastating a small village of strawberry cup cakes.

Silas slowly got to his feet. The books could be cleaned up although he winced as he noticed the bent pages in his Francois LeRoque volume. He had already photocopied every page so he knew the recipes inside out, it's just the principle of the thing. The culinary master had only ever completed one slim volume of his legendary recipes before dying tragically in a disastrous garlic seafood poisoning incident in downtown Paris.

Silas bent down to pick up the fragments of his shattered oriental porcelain book end. There was no repairing it this time he thought as he gazed at the broken fragments. To his surprise, however he noticed that the heavy red dragon had in fact been hollow and that a faded piece of parchment had been released from within.

He picked it up. At first the confusing Chinese letters made no sense to him but as he stared at them, almost held by some mystical force, the script began to dance in front of his eyes. After what seemed like hours, he somehow understood what it was. This was ancient Chinese wish-paper.

Many years ago in ancient China, a famous wizard and alchemist was forced to serve an evil emperor who was himself a master in the darker side of magic. The great wizard could do nothing to escape this wicked tyrant, even if he died, the powerful villain would simply bring him back. The only way he could escape was to lose his magic. So, one night he raised a terrible storm and cast a spell which sent all of his magic power in a letter, which he promptly posted to his wife the next day before the Emperor knew what had happened.

It is from small cuttings of this thousand year old letter that Chinese wish-paper is made. It is so enthused with the old wizard's power that it grants any three wishes to whoever finds it. But, the wizard only had minutes to complete what was one of the most complex spells in history so wish-paper is often as dangerous as it is powerful. Importantly, it will give the lucky finder exactly what they ask for.

So we now know that Chinese wish-paper works by magic. It is neither good nor evil, it simply is. You just need to think your wish and the powerful magic in the paper will make it come through. This was Silas's big chance.

Silas clenched his eyes shut and tried to empty his thoughts. He needed to get this one right. Before he could even review the most common wishes, two images flashed into his mind stronger than any other. It was Elvis Presley and Marilyn Monroe. That was it. Of everything in the world, he wanted to meet these two legends for dinner. Elvis would regale him with tales of the music industry and Marilyn had been his first and biggest crush. Two wishes completed before he even had a chance to draw breath.

Silas instinctively dropped the paper and opened his eyes. Nothing notable had changed. He looked around the shop; no one there...

After a few minutes staring expectantly out of the cake shop window, Silas heard a knock at the back door. Well, not so much a knock, it was more of dull tap, tap, tapping sound. He ran through to the kitchen and looked through the misty glaze of the security door. Even through the frosted glass, it was surely the King. He could see that giant white collar and a sweeping black quiff even in the dim light of the backyard.

On opening the door, a strong waft of decomposition and rot swept into the cake shop. It was Elvis. In fact, it was exactly Elvis, brought back straight from his grave in Graceland. He had died in 1977 and must have been buried in his favourite white leather Vegas jumpsuit, the one covered in metallic sequins and with pointed lapels you could land a plane on. The bloated and waxy walking corpse in front of him bore some resemblance to the King of rock roll but his hair was too long, his face too drawn and sullen.

My God, thought Silas. as the lumbering King lurched forward through the door trying to grab him, *It's zombie Elvis!*

Instantly he panicked and struggled frantically as undead Elvis's hands clawed and ripped at his apron. As he broke free, Elvis seemed to moan a deep 'Ah-hah' from deep inside his rancid frame and launched a heavy leg forward into a Vegas show style kungfu kick. Despite being dead, the King clearly still had some moves.

The kick caught Silas on the back of his legs and sent him flying to the kitchen floor. He turned to see zombie Elvis lurching towards him, his mouth open and yellow incisors dripping with putrid milky foam.

Silas reached up and grabbed hold of his rolling pin. This was not the Elvis he loved. This was some ghoulish shell or imitation. It was soulless. The King had to go down. With this in mind, Silas swung his heavy wooden pin into the King's head. Part of Elvis's skull caved in and his outfit erupted into a shower of silver and gold sequins.

The King was clearly shaken by the impact but his piercing, ravenous eyes were soon alight again and his mouth was salivating at the thought of human flesh.

Thinking quickly, Silas pulled open the tall cold room he used to keep all of his fresh ingredients. As the undead King of rock'n'roll was gearing up for another powerful kungfu kick, Silas grabbed his gold bedecked hand and swung the walking corpse into the large fridge. Elvis was sent flying into piled cartons of eggs and milk. Silas slammed the door and jammed it shut.

Inside, the King emitted further deep tuneful groans as he hammered against the freezer door. The noise was surely going to be heard. Silas flicked the operating panel open on the refrigeration unit and turned it down to the lowest setting. The King would be frozen solid in about an hour. And, sure enough, the noise began to tail off, to be replaced a soulful long moan which sounded vaguely like Elvis's moody anthem 'In the Ghetto'.

My lord, thought Silas. He had almost been dinner for Elvis. The King was back for sure but back as he is now. A living dead King of rock'n'roll with an unhealthy appetite for human flesh, straight from the grave in Graceland.

Silas mulled over the amazing events of the evening so far. He stopped in mid-thought. He'd used two wishes. Where the hell was Marilyn Monroe, his supposed love interest?

He kept hold of his trusty rolling pin and looked into the darkness of the shop. Marilyn had been dead for years, she'd be worse than Elvis. Images of a dried skeletal figure with a withered face and faded white hair, flashed through his mind.

Silas could hear a dull munching sound coming from within the gloom of the shop. This wasn't going to be pretty. She'd gone in 1962—that's more than 4 decades in the grave.

To his surprise, on the turning the lights on, he saw a shapely female figure with her back to him, standing over the éclairs counter. She was muttering 'hungry, so hungry' in the cutest American accent Silas had ever heard, even though her voice was muffled as she jammed in cake after cake.

Her hair was still a lustrous platinum blonde and she was dressed in a stylish if dusty little black number. Maybe this wasn't going to work out as badly thought Silas.

The corpse of Marilyn must had heard him come in or noticed the lights coming on, as she slowly turned to face him. The sight that greeted him would be enough to put most people off chocolate éclairs for life. Her shrivelled, parched face was smothered in cream and chocolate. Part of one side seemed to have drooped down as she stared at him with loathsome undead eyes. 'Foooood' she murmured in the same sweet voice.

One thing for Marilyn, thought Silas as the blonde corpse lurched towards him, arms outstretched, *at least she had kept her figure*. But, apart from her radiant white teeth, the years buried in the grave had not been kind to the face. No spectral beauty here. This was as fouler a ghoul as one could imagine, with thin, almost translucent, skin stretched tightly over an all too visible skull.

As she stumbled forward, he caught her humming a wicked little tune he recognised and adding in the twisted words, 'happy re-birthday to me, happy re-birthday to me'. This was getting sick thought Silas. The creatures he had brought back were not the stars he loved, they were dangerous and vicious walking corpses.

As the ghoulish Marilyn was almost upon him, Silas closed his eyes and swung the rolling pin towards the decaying objective that had once been his fantasy woman. They locked in combat; Silas dodging each snap of the dried crone's bony jaws. Eventually Marilyn was sent flying into the kitchen and as she tripped, she banged her head savagely on the kitchen table and slumped to the floor. A great thick purple liquid oozed from her head. The platinum blonde wig the corpse had been wearing now lop-sided had revealed a bald, fungus spotted scalp underneath.

With zombie Elvis freezing safely in the fridge unit and ghoulish Marilyn knocked out on the floor, Silas sunk into a chair and took a deep breath. The shop was a mess; the kitchen looked like a bomb site. All of his fresh ingredients were jammed in the cold room with the dead King of rock'n'roll and the world's greatest pin-up was leaking embalming fluid onto his hygienic tile floor.

It was the night of the 22nd December, just a few hours before the start of the busiest two days in the cake making calendar. Silas felt like crying as he noticed his stack of carefully iced Christmas cakes battered and crushed in his battle with the zombies. The famished undead Marilyn had made short work of his remaining yuletide logs. *How could things possibly get worse?*

Just then he heard a heavy click from the kitchen. He looked up and Marilyn's body had gone from the floor. Then came a creaking swing and a low southern drawl with echoes of 'Burning Love'. The skeletal Monroe had managed to unlock the fridge door, releasing permafrost Elvis.

Silas had only just managed to fight them off one at a time, now he faced the two ghoulish legends as they pushed their way through the door into the shop. If it is possible for a ghoul to become angry then this would aptly describe these two figures. Frost covered Elvis sequinned white outfit, but his eyes blazed red with anger and malice. Marilyn had desperately tried to put her blonde wig back on but was having trouble straightening it with half of her head caved in. She had given up on the false teeth and bared her wicked looking sharp teeth in anticipation of feasting on human flesh.

Silas backed away from the two grisly ghouls as they forced him into a corner of the shop.

Suddenly Silas caught sight of the Chinese wish paper. Of course, he had one more wish. As he reached to grab it, Elvis chopped down his heavy arm to catch his human prey but Silas was too quick for the strong but half-frozen ghoul. He quickly snatched the wish-paper and pushed a pile of white cake boxes in to block the doorway.

Silas cleared his mind. This needed to be a good one and he only had a few seconds. However, in times of great stress, some people are prone to the worrying condition of a blank mind and so it was with Silas Cartwright. Once cleared, no useful thought would enter his empty head. The more he strained the more vacant he become. As the two ghouls approached, he flicked open his eyes.

The first thing he saw was his bent first edition of *Gateaux Royale* by Francois LeRoque. And before he had time to think another thought, the most French pastry chef of all time sprang into his mind. Thinking for his life, Silas just managed to tack onto to the end of his thought the phrase, 'on my side, always on my side'. And, the wish was complete. The Chinese wish-paper erupted into a bright magnesium style flame in his hand and burned out into smoky vapours. All three wishes used.

The ghouls easily broke through the boxes but paused on hearing something behind them. It was a sound akin to a squeaky cat and a joke French accent and upon turning around, they were greeted with a thin, wiry ashen-faced corpse in a dusty white chef's outfit. Thank god he wasn't cremated thought Silas, as he caught sight of his crusty helper.

The newly arrived Gallic ghoul quickly dropped into a classic boxing stance. He clearly meant to 'take out the trash' as they say in this fiery sport of gentlemen. Zombie Elvis and Marilyn turned to take care of this menace before feasting on Silas but as Marilyn rushed forward, she was greeted with a bony fist connecting sharply with her jaw. The dried out film star was sent crashing to the floor. A first round knock out to the dancing Frenchman.

The kungfu King of rock'n'roll would not be so easy and as the ghoulish chief floated in his old-fashioned Queensbury rules boxing stance, Elvis gyrated as best he could trying to land a devastating kick or chop on his undead opponent. Silas watched as the two zombies circled each other, Francois muttering some mocking French profanity and the King, humming a dry throaty version of the 'It's Now or Never'.

When alive, Elvis must have been a far bigger man than the musky French chef and now his bloated corpse was substantially larger and the overweight King began to gain the upper hand. Francois's well-aimed jabs hardly affected the bulky singer and it was only a matter of time before he landed a kick which could shatter the nimble corpse of the French chef.

Silas seized his chance. He lifted the heavy till from the side and whilst Elvis was pulling off his now legendry mock-dance poses, Silas smashed the metal till onto

Elvis' head. The King's skull was shattered and his body slumped to the floor. The surprising agile Francois wasted no time and rammed a hand-held whisk into Elvis's open skull. He drove the whisk for a minute or so until what was left of his brain was a delightful and light white milky mousse. He quickly did the same to Marilyn. 'Parfait,' he muttered as he completed the grim task.

Silas stood staring at the slim dried figure of the famous French chief. Here he was face-to-face with the greatest cake chief of all time. 'How may I help you my good friend?' asked Francois in his strong French accent. As he finished, he coughed up a handful of dirt. 'Excusez-moi,' he offered.

The two chiefs sat up talking for hours, long into the night. Francois had died in 1777 and soaked up everything he could about developments in the cake and icing industry in the last two centuries. He smiled as Silas showed him his first edition of the Francois' slim cooking volume.

After they had re-buried Elvis and Marilyn in the back yard, the two cleared up in the bakery. Silas hoped they never had any reason to exhume either of the bodies from their original tombs. Empty coffins - now that would really feed the conspiracy theories, he thought.

And as for Francois, well, unlike the other ghouls who returned with an unhealthy appetite for human flesh, the dandy French pâtissier came back only with a desire to bake and to create new and delicious cakes with all the modern utensils, tools and ingredients at his disposal. He needed neither work nor sleep, only the occasional can of dog food for energy. All he wanted was a concealed place to work, a new set of aprons and some long rubber hygienic gloves. In exchange, he created and baked like the tireless chef-corpse he was.

Whilst Silas slept that night, the great Francois was back in culinary action for the first time in two hundred years. When Silas came down stairs at five o'clock as normal, Francois had created over fifty brand new cakes, pastries and flans. The delicacy of the white icing on his twenty luxury Christmas cakes was truly the work of a great master in the sugary art of decoration.

Silas quickly re-stocked the shop with the new creations. The only things he left out were the collapsed fruit sponges François had incinerated in the microwave, a new technology he had taken a particular shine to.

Needless to say, when the doors opened, just a few regulars drifted in. Mrs Siddiqui picked up two of the new cherry-frosted tortes and François's new orange cupcakes soon emptied. But, it was after a few hours, as word spread that the bustling Christmas crowds started to pour in from all over town.

By the end of the day, the shop had sold out of virtually everything. Just François's risky Nut and Spam fusion sponge cake remained. Even geniuses make some mistakes, thought Silas.

The 23rd and Christmas Eve turned out to be the best sales day in the little shops history. Whilst Silas kept front of shop, the busy corpse of François in the kitchen baked and created twenty-four hours a day. As quickly as the CakenBake superstore copied one of the recipes, two more were created. Some such as the fluffy white chocolate soufflé cake; they were simply unable to copy.

In the new year, the dreary cake shop was renovated into a sparkling new emporium. Whilst Francois worked on Volume 2 and 3 of his greatest cake recipes, Silas Cartwright become the rich and successful man he had always dreamed off.

And, it is still said that on cold still nights in late December, in that dreary northern town, you can still hear the echoes of the King of Rock'n'Roll as he mumbles from beyond the grave. Well, a bit closer than that actually, as he is buried in the backyard of the sparkling new Bakers shop on Lower Medley Street.

THE EMISSARY GOAT
by Colin Fisher

The Emissary Goat

scapegoat (orig. escape goat)

noun   /skap/goat/

A goat sent into the wilderness after the Jewish chief priest had symbolically laid the sins of the people upon it, the Azazel goat was one of two goats chosen for the ceremony on the Day Of Atonement. The first goat was sacrificed, while the scapegoat was driven into the desert.

'and Aaron shall cast lots upon the two goats, one lot for the Lord and the other lot for Azazel. And Aaron shall present the goat on which the lot fell for the Lord, and offer it as a sin offering; but the goat on which the lot fell for Azazel shall be presented alive before the Lord to make atonement over it, that it may be sent away into the wilderness.' (Leviticus 16:7–10).

He hated going down the stairs, even with the light on.

He didn't like the hollow sound they made, and he didn't like to think about what lay under them - the hollow, empty belly of the theatre, full of old props, old sweat and the ghosts of old performers. Miss Jacobs told him he was fanciful, that the school was lucky to be allowed to use Markham's, with all its history and the tradition of famous thespians that had graced its boards. Adam didn't know about that, he just saw the torn and tatty seats, the faded posters of bygone triumphs in the lobby, and the bare threaded drapes that hung in dark folds at the side of the stage. Creaking winches shifted a cloud of must every time they were drawn. He didn't like the portraits in dusty glass, of white faced men with greased hair, and dark eyed women in flowing robes and ornate hats, desperate eyes looking down on a world that had forgotten them and their careers. He never saw them on tv. Everything about them was trapped in black and white. They lined the stairs like adverts on the underground, relics of a heyday that would never return, and meant nothing to him. They were creepy, and he tried not to look at them as he descended toward the prop room door, feet echoing on the worn wooden stairs.

His face burnt, whether through anger or embarrassment he wasn't sure. It wasn't so much Craig's comments as the way he said them, the smug dismissal and turning away before Adam even got a chance to reply. He thought Miss Jacobs at least would agree with him, not Craig. Just *once* couldn't he have a speaking part? Not even the main part—yes, he knew Craig's mum was Artistic Director at Markham's, and Craig was going to go to drama school and be a *proper* actor, and it was really nothing more than a 'suggestion' that, really, Craig should be considered for a lead role in all the school productions—not even the main part, just one with a bit of speaking and some action. This year Adam had told his mum that he had a good part in the school nativity play, one of the three kings, would maybe get a song on his own, and she was coming with dad—as if that wasn't a miracle in itself—and bringing nan and granddad too. Ok, so he probably *shouldn't* have told her, but he'd had that talk with Miss Jacobs saying how much he liked acting, and Old Mr Jones, who played the piano every year, had told her Adam had a really good singing voice. He was ninety-nine percent sure he was going to get the part of Balthazar. Ninety percent sure, anyway. And now this. Trooped out of the school, across the car park behind Sainsbury's, and round the back of the High Street to Markham's Palace Theatre with the rest of the class, just to stand in a line and be told he was playing 'a beast come to adore Jesus.' He didn't hear the first time. He'd been rehearsing Balthazar's lines in his head, '*We have crossed the desert, from India, Persia, and Arabia, bearing gifts unto him*', and he didn't realise his name hadn't been called, although all the speaking parts had. Then it was just Miss Jacobs handing out the badges saying 'Beast of the Stable' to the children who hadn't got Mary, Joseph, the Angels, the Innkeeper, the Three Kings or the Shepherds. Even Samantha Shaw, who never stopped sniffing and complained about even *being* in the play, got to be 'Christmas Star' and had a dance all to herself. He couldn't even register it, just stared at the cardboard label that had been pressed into his hands saying 'Beast' and looked along the line in shock to realise all the other parts had gone. He felt his stomach lurch and a wave of nausea wash over him. He had told *everyone* he had a speaking part, a big part, and his dad was taking the day off and driving up from Salisbury specially. He stood, while the others bustled about him in excitement, dragging props and painted scenery out of the boxes that had been brought up in Mr Jones' Land Rover, oblivious to his panic and the badge he held in shaking hands. Okay, he thought, okay. She's just forgotten. I'll sort it out. It'll be sorted out in a minute.

He stumbled forward, to where his teacher was counting out pages into neat piles, scripts waiting to be assigned to their lucky recipients. She glanced momentarily at him, and then licked her thumb and went back to her counting. 'Two for Angel One, Two for Angel Two, Two for Angel Three, Three for Mary, Three for Joseph,' She paused, hand hovering with a page that he knew should be his, and looked at him impatiently, 'Yes Adam, what is it? You're supposed to be helping Naima with the stable.' And she nodded at an out of breath girl struggling with two boards on which bales of hay had been painted. Adam frowned. 'Miss... '

'Adam, I'm *really* busy. I want to get one read through done before home time.'

He stood, trying to think what to say, but showing no obvious sign of going anywhere, and she sighed, and put down her pages, looking at him directly. 'What is it, Adam?'

'Miss. I thought... ' he hoped she'd guess what the problem was, what had gone wrong.

'What, Adam?' Suddenly she shouted 'Corinne, put that *down*. Wait for Mr Patrick, that's far too heavy.' Dropping the pages, she hurried across to relieve the

Irish girl of the front of the Inn before hurrying back and scooping up the scripts. She scribbled names on them with marker pen. 'I need to supervise, it will have to wait Adam' she said.

He looked at the names, solidly black on the marked scripts. 'It can't wait' he mumbled, 'It's a mistake.'

'What's a mistake?' She sighed, 'What have you done?'

'I haven't done anything, Miss.' He stared at his feet. 'You have. You made a mistake.'

To his intense embarrassment Craig chose this moment to wander over, on the pretext of getting his script, but in reality just because he was nosey. He was followed by Becky Forsyth, and Justin, and Aaliyah, and soon Adam had all of Craig's adoring acolytes as an audience. Miss Jacobs spoke to him while handing round the scripts, 'Well, Adam, what is it? What mistake?'

'What's a mistake, Adam?' said Craig, 'what is it? We've got a play to put on.'

Adam considered saying 'nothing', and just slinking back to his place in the group, but he knew this was his one chance to sort everything out. 'I thought... I thought' he said in a small voice.

'Can't hear you Adam,' said Craig, 'What is it? What's the problem?'

'That's enough Craig,' said Miss Roberts, 'just concentrate on your lines.' She raised her voice 'Everyone over there for the read through.' The scene shifters hurried to where she pointed, but the small group around Adam gave no sign of having heard. She looked down at Adam again, 'Well?'

'I thought I was going to be a king. I thought I was Balthazar.' He said in a rush. He looked down at the cardboard label in his hands, 'You've given me 'Beast' by mistake.'

'That's right,' she said, looking at her list, 'Beast of the Stable, come to adore Baby Jesus.' That's you, Thomas, Zoe and Holly. Balthazar is... ' She rifled her papers, 'Kevin.'

'But Kevin can't sing,' he said desperately, 'I can sing, Mr Jones said I could sing really well. You said you'd consider it.'

She frowned 'I did? Well... I did. And I solved the problem because Melchior is going to sing instead, which is Cameron, and he has a wonderful voice.'

'Come on Adam,' smirked Craig, 'You'll make a great Beast. Just crawl around on all fours. Moo!' Everyone laughed, and Adam felt his face starting to redden.

'That's enough, Craig, back to your place. Adam, I'm sorry, but not everybody can get a song.'

'Just a speaking part... ' he said desperately, not caring that he was starting to plead.

Craig laughed nastily 'Isn't 'moo' speaking?'

'Craig, that's *enough*.' Miss Jacobs was starting to look flustered. 'Come on everyone, we must get started.'

'Why doesn't Adam get one of the old costumes out of the prop store?' Said Craig suddenly 'He'll look a proper beast then. No one will be able to see him.'

Adam wanted to punch him, but Miss Jacobs paused, 'That's not a bad idea.' She looked Adam up and down, 'Could look really authentic. We've had lots of good stuff out of there in the past. Adam, pop down and see if there's anything that would do for an animal.'

'But I won't even be seen!' Adam wailed, thinking of his whole family sitting with their cameras, and his mum and dad at opposite ends of the row, but still equally proud of their son. 'That's no good!'

'Just pop down and have a look,' she said, 'I'll send Mr Patrick down to help when he arrives.'

Craig and his little group of fans were turning away, as if dismissing Adam from everything important. Without even looking at him, Craig said 'No-one needs to see *you*, Beast, they're coming to see proper actors.' And to a general chorus of laughter he hurried away to take up his rightful place as star of the show, leaving Adam to trudge miserably over to the stairs, with tears pricking at his eyes, and his face flaming red.

He paused at the foot of the stairs. His embarrassment was draining out of him, as the anger took over. He wanted to go back up and tell Craig what he thought of him, and his mum's horrible old theatre. Everyone hated it anyway, that's why it was closing down. The children enjoyed scaring each other with tales of its haunted past. Two deaths, which became ever more gruesome with each telling; an accident on stage with a prop a hundred years ago, and a stagehand found dead one morning, stabbed in the back. Other injuries, rumours that all contributed to its unlucky reputation. Most of it was nonsense, Adam was sensible and knew that, but it was difficult to dismiss it all when he stood down here at the bottom of the stairwell, alone. The sound of the class getting ready, laughter and running feet, drifted down, but seemed muted, cut off. An ancient actor stared down at him from behind cracked glass, bearing an expression of mock terror. The legend 'Freddie Fear, He's Afraid of Everything!' ran in jagged letters underneath. His mouth was a horrible black O of astonishment. Adam shivered, and felt as if the wrinkled comic could see some hideous future looming over him. With an angry scowl—well, *he* wasn't afraid of everything—he turned the handle, and pushed the door to the prop room wide.

He expected it to creak, but it opened on well-oiled hinges, shedding a pool of light into the dark space. Adam stepped forward into the stale smelling room, fumbling on the wall to his right where he knew the light switch lay. He flicked it on, and one bare bulb shone down on the jumble of boxes, folded drapes, and strange unidentifiable costumes that filled the huge space. He could tell immediately that there was little illumination beyond the circle he stood in, the other bulbs gone or blown. Briefly, he contemplated going back up or waiting for Mr Patrick, but he knew what Craig and his cronies would have to say about that, and he decided he'd rather make a start digging through the old props and dusty scenery.

He started off down an aisle to his left, between rows of stained jackets hanging on metal racks. He pushed them aside, wheels creaking as they slid away from him to bump into other piles strewn haphazardly against the wall. There was so much *stuff*. Cases full of masks and faded robes, velvet dresses and frilled shirts, old furniture, tables, high backed chairs with torn seats and broken legs, wicker baskets with worn leather straps, and things that looked like the sort of instruments he'd seen in the school laboratory—glass bowls, racks of test tubes, and ceramic dishes. There were hats of all shapes and sizes, and he contemplated putting one on, but thought of the pictures on the walls, and who might have worn them years ago, and decided he didn't want to. There were common, everyday items that just looked old like telephones and odd looking radios with dials and numbers instead of digital displays, so he couldn't tell if they were props or had belonged to the theatre, and just been thrown down here when they no longer served a purpose. It seemed to be that kind of place, the place where old, useless relics fell through the cracks in the building's memory, to end up covered in dust and drapes and darkness. Halfway down the room he came to a case with the hilts of stage weapons sticking out, and he pulled out a sword and swung it to and fro for a few seconds, but he didn't like the sticky handle, or the way it clung to his skin when he moved his fingers. He dropped it back in the box with an expression of disgust, wiping his hand on what looked like an old policeman's jacket, and continued on his way, pushing aside boxes, and lifting away the refuse of a hundred productions, all the while trying to find something suitable to take back upstairs into the light.

He hoped he wouldn't find anything. Even if he didn't have any lines and his mum and dad and nan and granddad were going to be disappointed, he still didn't want to be covered up. Then it really would be pointless them coming. He was already coming up with an 'I'll show you' plan. What if he *did* say something? Just a line, no-one would be able to stop him or tell him off if he waited until the real performance. If the Star of Bethlehem could have a stupid dance, an animal could have a line. He could be the leader of the animals in the stable, the spokesperson —well, spokesanimal—so why *shouldn't* he have a line? Didn't Jesus deserve it? Couldn't God magic up a talking animal so the beasts could praise his son as well?

Pleased with his flash of brilliance, and with his eyes now becoming accustomed to the gloom, Adam returned to his hunt with renewed enthusiasm.

He reached the back of the prop store without having met with any success. Leaning against the wall was a collection of scenery flats. Adam could see green hills on one, and behind it what looked like bare yellow heights of sand dunes reaching up to a smouldering red sky. He didn't like either of them, or the others he could see lining the wall—tall buildings with empty windows, or seascapes with dark, roiling waves. They all looked unfriendly, unreal. He could imagine painted faces hidden in the darkness, behind the dunes or in the unseen rooms of flat houses. Motionless, two dimensional people with bright clothes and fixed expressions, still, listening. Looking out at their audience and wishing they were unreal too.

Adam shivered, and was about to turn away, when he noticed the costumes. An assortment of animals was jumbled among the scenery. There were blankets painted like hides, with brown and white patches, or spots, or stripes, or the woolly fleece of sheep. He could see two monkey costumes, with ragged black hair, and behind them the rubbery, scaled skin of a crocodile. He could also see animal heads stacked against the wall, and he approached them reluctantly, still not entirely happy with the idea that he would be concealed from view.

He became even less happy as he began to pick through them. Most were paper mâché; stiff and hard, but all had seen better days, with holes like wounds and sallow yellow skin. Crude lips and teeth had been drawn upon them, making them look like mummies he had seen in textbooks, their faces stretched tight and lips shrivelled from broken molars. They wouldn't be any good, he was certain, and he didn't want to try them on anyway. There was a cow, but there was no way he was wearing that after Craig's comments, and a sheep that had a fist sized hole in its nose. A scowling pig's head with cavernous eyes like pits leant against a bucket, but there was a wooden apple jammed in its mouth, and he didn't think it would be suitable for Baby Jesus' stable. Apart from that there were just dogs, fierce and desperate, a cat with no jaw, and a crocodile head. None looked likely to be at home in a stable in Bethlehem. The rest were just a stack of paper masks, with nothing more elaborate than whiskers to add a touch of authenticity.

Adam sighed, and was just turning away when he caught sight of another head, lying half hidden in the shadows of the weird desert scene. The seascape leaned at an angle across it, and he had to kneel down and crawl between the two to get at it. He crouched on his haunches, and examined it in the shaft of light.

It was a goat, more solid and realistic than the other masks. He didn't know what it was made of, but it was a good replica, not like their stiff dried paper. It had hair, a bit mangy and grey, but realistic (and the thought occurred to him that either someone had done it all by hand, or it had real goatskin stretched over it) and ears made of some silky fabric. A small beard jutted from its jaw, and it stared up at him with glass eyes, dark and mysterious. Best of all was the horn that spiralled up and out from its brow. It looked imposing and majestic, threatening even, although the other was missing. There was what appeared to be a patch of torn hair around the hole, edges ragged and stained a dark colour. It was a shame, but he didn't mind as it looked as if it had been in a life or death struggle. He began thinking about his character, the close escapes from desert nomads, or brushes with Herod's hungry soldiers, out hunting for the Firstborn. It would give him some background, like a *proper* actor.

Adam upended the head and looked inside the hollow space. It seemed to be supported by a wire frame, and there was a vague smell he couldn't place. Not nasty, just... different. It smelt like the spices his mum sometimes used for her more exotic dishes, the ones she cooked when her boyfriend Tony came to tea. Carefully, Adam lowered the mask over his head, and breathed in slowly, as if venturing into some new and dangerous environment.

He was surprised how comfortable it felt. It was a perfect fit. It sat on his head snugly, and didn't move or chafe. The glass eyes seemed to be in the perfect position for him to see through, and although they had looked dark and opaque from outside, he found that he could see out of the head clearly when he looked at the other costumes. In fact, it was so comfortable he didn't feel in any hurry to take it off again. He wanted to think about his character some more.

He slid down the wall and sat, hands gripped around his knees. Where had he come from? How long had he walked across the desert, stones hurting his feet, burning by day and freezing by night, to reach the poor stable in Bethlehem? Not welcome though, never welcome.

I am the Goat of Azazel. I am the weight of your sins; I have borne them about my head, and walked without remorse on the stony pasture.

Hmm. Was that right? It sounded right. The words were in his head, and they seemed to have always been there. He heard them, but, in a way, he also remembered them. He remembered the taste of the wild nabak, its sweet fruit bursting in his mouth, and the scratch of the kaff el-Deb; more common, but less satisfying. Harsher, like the pitiless East that was his home.

I have stood by your temple, beaten by sticks. I have held curses, murders, adulteries. I have watched my brother die, and my Lord forsake me. This is your prophet, they have told me, as their blows rained down. I am bound on high with scarlet, and my limbs are shattered.

Yes, he remembered them. That was definitely it. He breathed slowly, and breathed in rhythm with something else, the head whose words came and went like dust, laying a film of image upon him.

I am the Goat of desolation, driven from the Mount. I am hate. O Lord, I have acted iniquitously, trespassed, sinned before you. And I have seen this, and it was good.

Adam felt calm, tranquil. He didn't feel upset, or embarrassed, now. He was better than Craig. Craig thought he was an actor, but he didn't know about real performing. He didn't know about the drawing of lots between who should die, and who should be driven into the wilderness, to exculpate impurity, sin, evil. Year after year, the weight accumulating in a never ending ritual. Ancient but ageless. Driven out, into the silence, paying for the sins of others, while they stood and cheered. That was how it always was, walking away broken while others remained whole. Oh my father. Didn't Craig realise who he was dealing with? Didn't Craig realise he would come back? He had been made for just such a task. The dead weight of sin lay like a cross on his shoulders.

Hear me, o ye Children. I am tragos apopompaios, the Goat Sent Forth. I am caper emissarius, the Emissary Goat. I have been turned away from God, and supped with fallen Angels. On the tenth day of the seventh month, I shall come to ye, and I shall go forth, Scapegoat, my teeth stained with your prayers, and your sins about my neck.

Craig was nothing. Less than nothing. Adam had borne the weight of a nation's sins for hundreds of years. All its murders, atrocities, wars and heresies. There was no crime, no evil, which he had not endured and taken away into the desert, among the scorpions and empty silence. Year after year, century after century, the fuel of incontestable suffering, the murmur of the dying and the damned. It had made him strong. Much stronger than those who had sent him, beaten and broken, out under the blinding sun. How could he not hate them, how could he not do evil? It was his role, what he was made for.

Adam crawled on all fours back along the tunnel between the scenery. As he did, his hand closed about something hard, ridged, pointed. It was his missing horn, torn away in the struggle the last time he had done this, the last time he had walked back out of the wilderness into the pitiless light. He trod the world always, fuelled by their anger. He had dwelt down here for a long time, occasionally stirring, occasionally thirsting under the red desert sky, hidden from the sun he detested. Yes, there had been deaths, killings. Accidents on stage. But they never thought of him, never thought of the old goatskin mask, dried skin from a ritual slaughter stretched over a thin wooden frame, horns still marked with the red thread of sin. For hundreds of years He had travelled Europe with circus performers, theatre troops, fortune tellers and occultists. Passing from hand to hand, his sins a catalogue of their failures, until his reward, until his rest. Adam hefted what he had found, felt its weight lovingly. Dry blood caked like dust between its whorls, the tip as sharp as it had ever been. It was time to take up his burden, and walk.

I am hunger. I am blood. The desert wind is less bitter than I.

Craig said people didn't want to see him. Craig didn't want to see him. Alright, he wouldn't. He wouldn't see anything, ever. Let's see if they wanted a Joseph without any eyes.

Oh my father, why hast thou forsaken me?

With his head back in its rightful place, and his horn held safely behind his back, Adam walked toward the illumination that streamed from the open door. His goat's mouth curled upwards in a smile.

Even with the light on, he loved going up the stairs.

SATAN VS SANTA
by Colleen Chen

The Grandmaster of the Reptilians yawned, balancing a scaly head on the point of his fist. Bulbous yellow eyes, whose gaze had made many a victim squirm, now threatened only to close. In his gladiatorial arena before him, two blue-skinned Zeta Reticulans were fighting a spidermonster, and the crowd was making clicking noises and flicking their tongues in and out of their mouths, signs of middling appreciation. The spidermonster had removed a leg from one of the Zetas, but the two comparatively tiny humanoids had taken off two of *its* legs, using them to gouge out its eyes, one at a time. Those sneaky Zetas! You never could trust them, thought the Grandmaster as he tried to maintain interest.

The truth was that the Grandmaster's gladiatorial games on fourth-density Mars were getting stale. He was tired of watching the same old gray aliens fighting Nordic aliens and small hairy dwarves fighting spidermonsters. He called up a nanoparticle projection of the nearest populated planets in all densities, seeking, as he often did, possible candidates for a more interesting fight.

His gaze fell on the neighboring blue planet, Earth. He was used to bypassing Earth in his search, as those soft and rabidly emotive humans were never much fun in the arena, but then something caught his eye. A dot was moving across Earth's sky in the nighttime part of the world. It was an old man in a red suit riding a reindeer-pulled sleigh. Every few moments he would grab a sack and jump down, landing on chimneys and sliding down with an acrobatic dexterity that belied his obesity. In a wink he'd be out again, running over rooftops to descend another chimney, and on until his sack was empty. Then it would be back up to the sleigh to a different neighborhood.

What was in those sacks? The Grandmaster's curiosity itched at him. It had been a long time since the Reptilian had been materialistic, given that he was a fourth-density creature and the physical realm was so passé. But he still loved surprises—and that passion was what drove these games. He pushed the projection into magnification, aiming to see what the old man had left in that little house right there...

He pushed too far. He found himself looking deep in the bowels of the Earth. Around the molten core were ledges of land, each crawling with toiling humans. Some were carrying rocks up hills. Some were swimming in lakes being chased by monsters with teeth as long as swords. Some were pinned up on crucifixes, being used as target practice by squat gray creatures holding needle-edged stars.

On the topmost ledge closest to the core stood a red-skinned man with horns and a forked tail. He was cackling while he whipped a line of men, forcing them to leap into an enormous bonfire. The Grandmaster chuckled and flicked his tongue out a few times. He hadn't known Earth had such enterprising residents.

He sat there for a moment, scratching his head. He was so lost in thought that he didn't even notice that the game was over. It was a satisfying ending, the spidermonster disemboweled with its own amputated legs, one of the Zetas dead and the other nearly so. When the Grandmaster's attendants brought in a cocktail made from fermented Martian beetles so he could relax after the match, he waved aside the drink and pointed to the projection.

'I want two Earthlings for a Game,' he said. 'The fat man who flies in a sleigh pulled by animals. And this red-skinned horned one who lives underground and likes to punish humans.'

The fourth density had no weekends, or even a strong concept of time, but when the match was scheduled the arena was packed and the vibration was of a Friday night party. Fresh sand glittered on the arena grounds, and aliens and monsters screamed and rattled the bars of the cages that lined the edges of the circle.

The Grandmaster fired a shot from his plasma gun into the air. Two of the cages squealed open.

Santa stumbled out of one cage, prodded forwards by a Reptilian with a plasma rifle. His eyes were puffy and dark-circled, as if he'd been up all night working. His suit was covered with soot and cobwebs. He looked anything but jolly.

Satan strutted out of the other cage, wearing nothing but a loincloth of gold lamé. He puffed out his chest, flexing one rippling red bicep as he held his pitchfork aloft. The crowd went wild, and Satan touched one of his horns and then gave the devil's salute.

When the two stood ten feet apart in the center of the arena, the Grandmaster leaned over the balcony.

'Greetings, Earthlings,' he said. 'We are honored you have volunteered to fight. You are both allowed to use whatever weapons and powers you can manifest. The match will end with one of your deaths. The winner will gain, of course, our approval, and will be allowed to leave with a great gift—his own life.'

'You'll have to offer something better than that,' scoffed Satan. 'We're both immortal, you stupid lizard.'

The Grandmaster made a motion with his hand, and the Reptilian guard standing behind Satan shot him with the plasma rifle. Satan grabbed his right buttock and howled.

The Grandmaster chuckled. 'As you should know from your own activities in Earth underground, even the supposedly immortal can suffer. So make each other suffer. And the one who does a better job will be the winner. The loser—well, you can say goodbye to ever seeing your little Earth again.'

'I am a peaceful man,' said Santa, his deep voice resonating through the arena. 'And I'm also very busy. It's Christmas Eve, and I have to get back and finish delivering presents, or many good little boys and girls will be sad tomorrow morning.'

'Then you have something to fight for, don't you?' the Grandmaster said.

'I won't fight!' Santa insisted.

But Satan grew excited at the thought of Santa being trapped on Mars, and never again another Christmas. What a fertile ground Earth would be for his evil! Without a word, he charged, aiming his pitchfork at Santa's protruding belly.

Santa would have been skewered, but the pitchfork hit his heavy metal belt buckle. 'Ow!' Satan yelled, dropping the pitchfork. He shook his numbed arm and glared at Santa.

The crowd made noises of derision, (however it is Reptilians do it), and some of them threw bits of molted skin at the pair. 'Pathetic!' they yelled, and even though it was in a language neither contender understood, the meaning was clear. Santa didn't care, but Satan was wild with offended honor. As Santa began a lumbering run around the arena, Satan followed him, red streaking after red.

Santa, huffing and puffing, pulled a reindeer bell out of his pocket and shook it. Faint jingling from the skies answered it, and a string of reindeer pulling a sleigh driven by two elves burst into view, heading straight for Santa.

'Wreath!' shouted Santa, and an elf pulled a Christmas wreath out of a sack and tossed it to Santa. Santa caught it and threw it like a discus. It fell over Satan's head and shoulders, pinning his arms to his body.

The sleigh landed, and Santa began to climb in. But Satan clenched his fists, and the wreath burst into flames. He threw the burning leaves at the sand beneath the reindeer's feet, and the reindeer reared and jumped into the sky; Santa didn't quite make it into the sleigh and tumbled onto the flames.

Santa's suit caught fire, and the old man rolled. His blackened suit fell off when he got up, leaving him naked except for a pair of red and green boxers.

But the sack had fallen out of the sleigh, free of the flames. Santa grabbed it and began to throw Christmas ornaments at Satan's head, hoping to knock him out. Centuries of delivering presents to all the children in the world in only one night had given Santa the ability to move at nearly lightspeed, and the crowd hissed in amazement as his arms were a pale peach blur, grabbing and tossing ornament after ornament.

Satan staggered, unable to see, his head a glittering mass of balls, lights, and small baby Jesuses. But he whistled shrilly, and Cerberus, his three-headed hound, went through a secret wormhole in Earth's Hell to Mars' Hell, and he came bursting up from the ground. Three licks cleaned the ornaments from Satan's head, and then Cerberus began to play catch with the rest of the ornaments Santa threw, eating them all.

'Hail!' screamed Satan, throwing his arms up towards the sky, and balls of ice the size of the Grandmaster's fist began to pelt the arena. Cries of wonder rippled through the spectators, who had never before seen snow.

'Locusts!' A dark cloud appeared over the sands, and insects fell down so thickly that it was Santa's turn to be blinded. Cries of appreciation came from the crowd now, and they began to run around, grabbing handfuls of tasty snacks from the sky. There had never been such a fight as this!

'Succubi!' shrieked Satan, and from the hole in the ground Cerberus had made, alluring demon women dressed in red velvet bikinis and Santa hats emerged, wading through locusts to undulate their way towards the near-naked fat man batting ineffectually at locusts and trying to avoid being skulled by hail.

'Wow,' breathed thousands of Reptilians in unison, as they ate locusts and stared at the succubi, mesmerized. It had been centuries since they'd felt sexual stimulation, but as succubi are *very* sexy, dusty libidos creaked to life, and cold blood began to warm.

The succubi surrounded Santa, pressing unholy curves against him and running nails down the rolls of his body. 'Can I sit on your lap and tell you what I want for Christmas?' one of them breathed. Santa's boxers couldn't hide the fact that he was getting distracted, and Satan, smirking, moved in for the kill.

But Santa muttered, 'Mrs. Claus, Mrs. Claus,' like a mantra. He grabbed a piece of hail and shoved it into his boxers to cool himself down. Then he called forth Christmas doves carrying industrial-strength umbrellas, and they cooed *Singin' in the Rain* as they kept the whole arena free of hail. The spectators were taking care of the locusts, filling their mouths and their pockets with the bounty from the skies. Then two elves leaped out of a swooping sleigh. Since Santa had already lost interest, the succubi were happy enough to switch allegiances, and soon a dust cloud arose around the mini-orgy, velvet bikiniwear and elf worker suits flying.

Amidst the mayhem, Santa and Satan came face to face. Satan smiled. 'Your time has come, old man. We've always known I'm stronger than you. You try to bribe people to be good, but even so, they still turn to me. You're just too soft to know how to win a game.'

Satan's pitchfork appeared in the air, and he caught it neatly, raising it to smash into Santa's face.

Santa opened his sack and took out a large box wrapped in shiny gold paper. 'Before you do that, here's something for you. Merry Christmas, Satan.'

'For me?' Satan paused. The arena was so chaotic, he could put off his moment of glory for just a bit. He dropped the pitchfork and sat down. He ripped off the wrapping paper and opened the box. Inside was a music box that looked like Earth. Satan wound it, and it played the tune to *He's Got the Whole World in His Hands*.

'I've never gotten a Christmas present before,' Satan said, a tear trickling down his cheek as he listened.

'You never asked me for one,' said Santa.

'I n-n-never thought I d-d-deserved one, because I've never been g-g-good!' bawled Satan.

'He's yours for the killing,' yelled the Grandmaster. He was jumping up and

down in his balcony with frustrated rage, shaking his fists, eyes bulging so hard they were pulsing. 'Finish him!'

'Everybody has a little bit of good in him,' Santa said, and he reached out and helped Satan, still clutching his gift, to his feet. Overcome, Satan threw his arms around Santa, and they hugged.

One of the interesting things about the fourth density is that thought-forms, especially those tied to powerful emotions, easily manifest in the physical realm. Now Reptilians are highly advanced mentally, but emotionally they're repressed. So Mars had never seen a moment such as the one Santa and Satan now shared. The light of that moment of love beamed out into a million sparkling little hearts with cherries on top, with angels singing to boot. Balls of ice melting in dents of sand turned into sunflowers, locusts turned to popcorn, and the succubi-elf orgy turned into something more resembling loving polyamorous play.

The Grandmaster screamed, shielding his eyes and his ears from all that love, and he stumbled and fell off the balcony into the cage of a giant spidermonster. His shrieks were quickly cut short, while the Reptilian spectators stood in hushed awe.

Satan only pulled out of Santa's embrace when he felt something tugging at his loincloth. It was a Reptilian child. It pointed to the popcorn and sunflowers and made a face, then pantomimed a flying insect, and made eating motions.

Satan shook his head. 'Locusts are only for when you've been bad,' he said. 'I think... I might just try being good now.'

Large lizard tears spilled from the child's eyes. Satan sighed and snapped his fingers. Locusts rained down again. 'Merry Christmas, then,' he said. The child squealed with delight and began to catch the falling insects.

Santa was smiling. 'Satan, it looks like you might have gotten yourself another job.'

'I've got a job though. I cause mischief on Earth,' Satan said.

'Ever heard of delegating work? Come on, Satan. Look at how happy you can make these folks. It's time for a change.'

Satan looked around at the arena full of ecstatic Reptilians. 'You're right, Santa,' he said. 'I'm going to do it!'

That day marked the first Martian Christmas. Santa helped Satan set up a second home at the Martian North Pole, where they built a factory for making nasty gifts to bring joy to all the bad little Reptilians in the fourth density. Fortunately, because time and space are not the same in the fourth density, after a long night partying Santa arrived back on Earth in plenty of time to finish delivering gifts.

'Ho ho ho,' Santa said, as Christmas Day dawned upon Earth. He looked up to see the fading twinkle of Mars. 'And a Merry Christmas to all!'

ALL HOLIDAY SPECIAL WITH MAGRITTE
by Brandon Cracraft

I remembered watching *Pygmalion's Friends* late at night on some kid's educational channel. A human actor taught history and life lessons through the use of puppets that were supposed to be statues that he brought to life using magical paint. The show was enjoyable but it dated really badly with its seventies hair styles and psychedelic soundtrack.

When hipsters stared wearing tee-shirts and boxer shorts with the Pygmalion's Friends logos and characters on them, Fenwick Studios decided to resurrect the franchise. They originally wanted to do a modern series, updating all the characters and adding computer animation. Focus groups told them that what attracted people to the series was the old puppets.

I pitched them a holiday special. The classic characters could meet people from different faiths and tell kids about the different winter holidays around the world. I figured that they didn't like the idea when I didn't hear from them in over a month.

Lily Cheung called me the day after I finished shooting an iced tea commercial where everyone spontaneously found themselves transported to the old South whenever they took a sip. 'We love your idea, Mr. Fitzpatrick. I have been in contact with one of the original puppeteers, Ronald Robinson. He played the little boy, Magritte, in the show. He agreed to reprise his role. If you are still interested, I expect you to meet us at seven o'clock tomorrow morning. Wear that burgundy blazer that you wore at the pitch. Some of the other producers didn't like it, but I thought it was whimsical.'

'Thank you, Ms. Cheung,' I said.

'Do not thank me yet, Mr. Fitzpatrick. You could still screw this up. Your only experience has been directing commercials, one of them for men's underwear, two for soft drinks, and a final one for skateboards.' She paused for a second. 'It is probably good that you worked with children.'

'Thank you,' I said. 'I also just finished a commercial for iced tea. I worked a lot with effects and costumes.'

There was a pause, and I wondered if I should say something else. 'I was simply listing your accomplishments, not paying you a compliment. Just remember, we can still replace you as director even if we use your idea.'

Instead of sleeping, I spent the entire night watching episodes of *Pygmalion's Friends* and researching various holidays. I scribbled a bunch of notes down and drank an insane amount of coffee in the hopes that I could type more than two sentences without a typo. When that was done, I tore through my closet trying to find the right outfit that managed to say both professionalism and whimsy. After my third change of socks, I swallowed a glass of orange juice and grabbed a handful of cereal.

Lily Cheung only stood four and a half feet tall, so she wore platform heels and a terminal amount of hair spray to give her a little height. 'Jeans and white tie,' she remarked, 'not the worst choice you could make.' I decided to take that as a compliment. 'I should warn you that there were some complications with Ronald Robinson.'

'He couldn't make it?' I asked, suddenly aware that I never took the time to brush my teeth. 'Is he in the middle of filming something else?'

Ms. Cheung shook her head. 'Mr. Robinson arrived early. According to him, he's always early. In fact, I think it would be best if he explained the situation to you directly.' She opened the door. 'He likes to be called Ronnie.'

Even though the man sitting at the end of the table was obviously around sixty years old, he moved and spoke like a little boy. 'I just wanted to say that I still think I can do it,' he stuttered out nervously. 'I mean, it hasn't gotten that bad. I mean, not yet. I might need a little TLC, but I swear that I can still do it.'

'My name is James Fitzpatrick,' I said, speaking to him slowly like he really was a child. I felt like a jerk as soon as I realized what I was doing. I hoped that my first impression didn't make me seem like a condescending prick. 'Is there something wrong, Mr. Robinson?'

'Ronnie,' he said, making a face. 'I hate it when people call me Mr. Robinson.' He fiddled with the papers and pens on the desk. I resisted the urge to take them from him. His light brown eyes quivered as he tried to make eye contact, so he started to look down at his lap. He was dressed in a suit at least two sizes too big for him, adding to his childish image. 'I just got diagnosed with early onset Alzheimer's disease.'

Ms. Cheung gave me a look. 'From what I have heard, it is a very minor case. He has problems with simple memory.'

'I know everything about Magritte, though,' he perked up. He grabbed the puppet and shoved him on his left hand and took at a small remote control for Magritte's eyes. I immediately forgot the middle aged man attached to Magritte. I actually started talking to the puppet.

'The thing is, Jimmy,' Magritte said. 'I really want to do this. I think it would be cool to talk about all these holidays. I never even heard of half of them.'

Ms. Cheung surprised me by speaking directly to the puppet as well. 'I actually contacted a Staff Sergeant Ahmed Zohar of the United States Marine Corp. He is excited to be talking about the Muslim Day of Ashura and the various ways that it is celebrated.' She let out a slight, lipless smile. 'He's doubly excited to meet you.'

'Jeepers!' the puppet screamed.

I extended my hand for the puppet to shake. 'I think we can work around any difficulties Ronnie has. We would love to have you both involved in our show. I'm calling it 'The All Holiday Special Starring Magritte.''

Magritte's eyes widened. 'Jeepers! Really, Jimmy?' You're going to name the special after me? I was in a Christmas special before, but they were always named after Pygmalion. You're the coolest, man! The absolute subzero coolest!' When I heard those lines in the show as an adult, I cringed. As a little kid, I loved every time that Magritte spoke in his fake French accent to hide the fact that he was born in the smoky mountains of Tennessee.'

After Ronnie and Magritte left, Ms. Cheung lit a cigarette despite all the non-smoking regulations. 'Are you sure about this, Mr. Fitzpatrick? He seems enthusiastic now, but this is a good day. If Ronnie truly has Alzheimer's, he will have bad days.'

'I think we can handle it,' I said. 'Beside I can't just fire that old man. He's been playing that character since before I was born.'

'Do you know who Captain Ahab is?' she asked. As typical for her, she didn't bother to wait for me to answer. 'Be careful not to go hunting white whale so quickly. Are you sure that you are willing to take care of Ronnie when he needs it?'

I shrugged it off. 'My mom and all of my sisters became nurses. I was raised around hospitals. I'm not afraid of someone just because he's a little sick. On that skateboard commercial, I worked with a fifteen year old boy that cried at the drop of a hat. I think I can handle Ronnie.'

The producer said nothing. She simply continued to smoke. Josh Lincoln, one of the college students she hired for a production assistant, told me that Lily Cheung only smoked when she was really nervous.

———

Ronnie Robinson gave such an amazing performance that no one noticed he wet his pants until I yelled 'Cut!' Sister Immaculate gasped when she saw the puppeteer's trousers were completely drenched. As far as I could tell, he didn't just have one accident but several. When everyone realized what he did, Ronnie started crying and ran off.

'Do you need my help?' Sister Immaculate said.

'No,' I said, 'I think I can handle it. Thank you for your time. That was the best telling of the Christmas story I have ever heard, and I went to Catholic school.'

I tried not to wince with disgust when he cleaved to me. 'I'm so sorry, Jimmy,' he said, crying into my bowling shirt. 'I wasn't paying attention. It's nothing I swear. I was just listening to that nun talk about the birth of Christ. I mean, I'm an old man. We have accidents. It doesn't have to mean that I'm going senile right now, does it?'

'Maybe you should wear some protection,' I suggested, 'Just in case you have another accident.' He looked at me. I thought about something I read about Alzheimer's patients. Sometimes they regressed back to a childlike state. I wondered if that was what was happening to Ronnie. 'I'll send Josh out to the drug store and buy you something. If you have an accident again no one will ever know.'

Ronnie nodded. 'Do you have kids, Jimmy? You act just like a father.'

'No,' I admitted. 'Maybe if I ever find myself a decent boyfriend, I'll try to adopt some or become a foster parent at least.'

'You remind me of my daddy,' he said. 'The two of us used to be really close before he killed himself.'

––––––––––

Everything seemed fine until the Wiccan priestess and her teenaged son showed up to talk about Yule. Meredith and Raven got along great with Magritte, and Ronnie seemed to really enjoy interacting with a kid again. The three of them sang old Irish tale that I'm pretty sure I heard my great-grandmother hum once or twice.

Raven looked a lot younger than his fifteen years, probably because he was so scrawny that on his pants he wore a little boy's belt decorated with superheroes just to keep them up. He dyed his hair dark green which looked nice against his half Apache features. 'It was great meeting you,' he told Ronnie.

Out of nowhere, Ronnie completely flipped out. 'He looks just like my son!' he kept repeating. 'He looks just like my son!' Ronnie ran off again, and Ms. Cheung shot me an impatient look.

When I caught up with Ronnie, he was hiding under a table and banging his head against the linoleum floor. 'He looks just like my son, Christian. My son always liked doing weird stuff with his hair.'

'I didn't know you had a son,' I said. 'I remembered seeing your daughter Maude on a couple of episodes of *Pygmalion's Friends* when she was a little girl.'

Ronnie let out a primal scream. 'This doesn't make sense, Jimmy. I can't remember where I put anything, but all these horrible memories keep coming back to me.' He slammed his head against the ground so hard that he drew blood. I managed to get him out from under the table and wiped the blood from his forehead. 'My son killed himself. It feels like it just happened yesterday.'

I never heard any of that. I checked his bio, and I never found any mention of his son. The internet told me all about his two ex-wives and his daughter's failed career as a singer before she became a puppeteer herself. Nothing about Ronnie even having a son, much less his tragic death.

'Can I go take a nap, Jimmy?' Ronnie asked. 'You don't need me until later tonight, right?' I helped him to his feet. 'I don't suppose that you could do me a huge favor, Jimmy. Can you tuck me in? It always makes me feel better when I get tucked in.'

I held my breath to keep from sighing. Ronnie was getting a lot worse. I hoped he could make it through the few days of filming.

Ronnie woke me up in the middle of the night. He walked down the hallway of the hotel in nothing but a tee-shirt and a pair of disposable briefs. His blanket trailed behind him like a wedding train. Once again, he looked like he was on the verge of tears. 'I kept having nightmares,' he said. 'I hoped that I could sleep with you.'

I pulled him into my hotel room before someone got a glimpse of him. 'Why didn't you put on a robe?' I asked. 'Do you really want people to see you like that?'

He completely ignored me and flopped down on my bed. 'I had a horrible nightmare about my daddy. Did I ever tell you how he died?'

I figured that it was best to just humor him. The shoot would be over soon enough. I made room for him on the bed then covered him with a blanket. 'I know that you told me that your father killed himself,' I said, 'same as your son.'

'Daddy sent me to the store to pick him up some cigarettes. Everyone smoked back then. He told me that it helped him with his nerves. We didn't know a lot about depression back then. When someone started acting weird and moody, people just said it was nerves. I came back from the store, and he took the pistol and shoved it down the front of his pants. He shot himself twice and then sat down in his favorite chair. I started screaming, but Daddy acted like nothing was wrong. He told me to sit on his lap. By the time he died, I was covered in head to toe in Daddy's blood, even my underwear was purple.'

'I'm sorry,' I said uncomfortably. I never knew how to react when people told me about disease or death. I tried my best to hide how nervous I was.

'It was worse with my son,' he continued. 'They knew something was wrong with Christian. They gave him a bunch of pills that was supposed to help. That's actually how he tried to kill himself. He swallowed the whole bottle. When he didn't die quick enough, he made himself a chocolate milk shake.' I swallowed, waiting for the kicker. 'He poured a bunch of oven cleaner in the shake. I guess he started literally vomiting his guts out. We found pieces of him around the house. The place was so full of blood that we had to move. None of us wanted to clean it up.'

'How old was Maude?' I asked. 'Was she older or younger than Christian?'

Ronnie looked at me confused. Finally, he said, 'I'm really tired.' He settled into bed and pretended to sleep, letting out snores so fake that they wouldn't fool a kindergartner. When he thought I was asleep, he whispered, 'Good night, Daddy.'

Ms. Cheung hired Fancy Taylor because she was the most recent winner of the one of the many reality show singing contests that I never watched. She fumbled with her Mrs. Santa Claus outfit trying to show more cleavage. 'My tits trended on twitter,' she said proudly. 'Maybe you could cut a hole in the top so I can show them off?'

'This is a kid's show,' I said.

'I'm really popular with boys eleven to seventeen,' she said. 'Besides, don't parents watch these shows with their children? Don't you want to give all the dads something to look at? And the lesbian moms? I'm popular with lesbians, too.'

Her version of 'Santa Baby' sounded like a porn parody of Betty Boop. I watched Josh Lincoln, my production assistant, cringe next to me. He handed me a note that called her 'Panty Claus.'

We used a lot of normal people. When Staff Sergeant Ahmed Zohar wished all of his 'brothers and sisters' in the Middle East a happy Day of Ashura, we all wanted to salute. A bunch of kids from a local Hebrew school told the story of Chanukah, being informative and adorable at the same time. Sister Immaculate taught kids how to phonetically sing a traditional Christmas song in Latin. Raven had all the charm of the 'quirky one' in a boy band to explain Wicca in a matter that wouldn't upset the Christian right. A bubbly J-Pop star explained the difference between Christmas in American and Christmas in Japan before breaking into her version of Jingle Bell Rock.

None of those people wanted to be actors. Fancy Taylor talked about how she was going to be in three different movies. Her acting was abysmal. She demanded a line read for everything but still delivered like she hit the bong between each sentence. The worst part is that she actually performed to Ronnie rather than Magritte.

'This just seems so stupid,' she said in the middle of a scene. 'Why does that have to be puppets? Couldn't we just use computer animation or something? I mean, puppets are weird.' She tugged on Magritte's ears. 'Look at this thing.'

'Don't touch him, you fucking bitch!' Ronnie screamed. He carefully pulled off Magritte before he began his temper tantrum. 'I've worked with a lot of shitty actresses, but you have to be the fucking worst!' He scurried over to me, grabbing my leg as he cried. 'I hate her, Jimmy. Please get rid of her. Please make the bitch go away.'

'You're all fucking crazy,' Fancy Taylor said. 'There's no fucking way that I'm staying here. I'm bigger than this little piece of shit. I could be doing a fucking movie right now with real fucking actors, not fucking puppets.'

She picked up Magritte and threw the puppet against the wall. Ronnie ran after him, picking up the puppet and cradling him in his arms. 'You bitch!'

'Fuck you!' she responded. 'I'm not fucking doing this shit.' She stormed off, flipping us off as she left.

Ronnie sat on the floor beside me, tears running down his face as he made sure that all the mechanics in Magritte still worked. 'I'm so sorry, Jimmy, but I can't work with her. You saw what she did with Magritte. Don't make me work with her, Jimmy, please.'

Ms. Cheung walked up to me and lit a cigarette. 'What do you want to do, Mr. Fitzgerald?' she asked.

I looked from Ronnie's pleading expression to the producer's judgmental one. 'We need a replacement,' I told Ms. Cheung. 'I don't want to work with her either. There has to be a better Mrs. Santa Claus than that slut.'

––––––––––––

The last time that Maude Robinson sang with her father she was thirteen years old. Her mother insisted that she train with professional vocal coaches and groomed her to join the opera. Maude wanted to be a pop star. Under the name 'Maudie Lynn' scored a top ten hit in 1988 with All Boys are Toys and sang I'm Not a Good Girl on the soundtrack of a teen sex comedy. Since then she appeared in three off Broadway shows and several touring shows and did a guest appearance on the same show that Fancy Taylor won.

Her version of Mrs. Santa Claus was the sweet old woman that invented snowmen and Christmas cookies. She treated Magritte like he was a normal little boy and managed to be motherly without ever talking down to the audience. My jaw dropped on the floor when she transformed Christmas carols I heard thousands of times into art.

'It was great singing with you again, Maude,' Ronnie said when it was over. 'I hope that the kids are doing well.'

Maude's cheerful Mrs. Santa Claus immediately faded. 'You could see them yourself if you ever started taking your pills again, Dad.' She put her hands on her hips and stared him down. 'I know that you're not taking them. I can see it in your eyes.'

'I don't want to talk about this,' Ronnie said. 'I sometimes forget to take my pills. It confuses me. Please, let's not talk about this.'

'He has his good days,' I said. 'Despite his Alzheimer's he always remembers his cues. What kind of pills is he taking?'

Maude gave me a confused look then her face twisted to anger. 'Alzheimer's?' she yelled at her father. 'You told them that you had Alzheimer's disease?' She turned to me. 'My father does not have Alzheimer's disease.'

'I hate to argue, ma'am,' I said as gentle as possible. 'He just got diagnosed with Alzheimer's. I've seen how it affects him. I might not be an expert on the disease, but I can recognize mental illness.'

Maude gave me a look that made me wonder if she was going to attack me. 'My father has delusional schizophrenia. He tells stories that he believes. He tells so many lies that he cannot figure out the truth. If he does not take his medication, his episodes can get pretty terrible. I remember being a little girl and finding all this blood over the house. Dad made a chocolate shake and put oven cleaner in it.'

'Just like your brother,' I said hushed.

'What brother?!' she asked, eying her father. 'I'm an only child.'

Everyone remained silent through the conversation. I told Josh to get everyone out. A couple of them actually made groans of disappointment. 'You never had a brother named Christian?'

'Christian is my father's real name,' Maude explained. 'He changed it to 'Ronald' after his father killed himself and he became an atheist.'

I stared at Ronnie in shock. 'There's no Christian?' I asked. 'You made him up.' Instead of answering, Ronnie ran out of the studio.

'You better go get him, Jimmy,' Maude said casually. 'There are a lot of things out there that he can hurt himself with. Trust me. I have seen what kind of damage that man can do himself with just a fork.'

Ronnie made it easy for me to find him. He decided to hide out in his hotel room. He left his door unlocked, so I knew the rustle under the bed was being made by him. He crawled into the furthest corner, making himself as thin as possible.

I searched for his antipsychotic medication, but I couldn't find any. After a while, I overturned his suitcases. When I grabbed the case he carried Magritte around in, he tore up his stomach trying to get out. 'What are you doing?' he whimpered. 'Please don't hurt him, Jimmy. He didn't do anything.'

'Have a seat.' I sat, patting the bed. Ronnie leaned close to me, and tried to work his way under my arm. 'We have one more day of filming. Please tell me that you can hold it together for one more day.'

Ronnie's face lit up. 'I promise, Jimmy.'

'Where are your pills?' I asked. 'I want to watch you take them.' He pulled away. 'I don't need any accidents, Ronnie. Where are your pills?'

Ronnie started pacing back and forth. I repeated the question, and he stomped up and down and kicked around the tables. 'I took my pills!' he said, using his most childish voice. He pointed to his throat. 'I took them all.' He threw an empty pill bottle at me. 'See. I took my pills, so you can stop yelling at me.'

I stood up and took out my cell phone. 'We have to get you to the hospital. You can't just take a full bottle of pills. You'll overdose.' He started to panic. 'Don't worry. I can shoot around you. I'll write some script about family and tradition. I did an underwear commercial with model Greg Hallaburton. He just got married to his boyfriend in New York and the two of them adopted twins. Greggie owes me a favor. I'll mix that with some extra footage of you, maybe some of the stuff with Fancy Taylor. The show will be fine.'

'But I want to go to the studio tomorrow,' he said.

I took his head in my hands and forced him to look at me. 'You took a bunch of pills. I don't know what that's going to do.'

'Make me better,' he suggested. 'The doctor told me that if I took the pills all at once than I would get better and never have to take them again.'

'That's not true, Ronnie. The doctor never said that. You just think he did, because you want him to have said that. You made that up like you made up your son Christian.' I started to dial 911, but Ronnie ripped the phone out my hand and smashed it.

'Stop that,' I said. 'We have to get you to the hospital.'

Ronnie's face became a mask of insanity. 'I don't want to go to the hospital, and you can't make me.' He smashed a mirror with his bare hands and I jumped. 'I'll get rid of those fucking pills.' He grabbed a shard of glass, cutting up his hand in the process. He started to rip into his throat. Blood squirted me in the eye. He sliced himself from chin to Adam's apple but thankfully missed the major vain. His shirt stained black. He smiled at me as he bled, preparing to slit his throat a second time.

'Stop it!' I yelled, too scared to move.

'Why?' he asked. 'I'm going to make everything better. When Daddy killed himself, he tried to make everything perfect for me. He said that everything was going to be perfect. Now I get to make everything perfect for my new daddy.' He kept babbling, but my shock muffled the sound.

'Listen,' I said. 'You need to be a good boy.' Ronnie looked at me sideways, his eyes bloodshot from all the drugs. 'I mean, it's almost Christmas. Don't you want to sit on Daddy's lap and tell him your Christmas list?' I sat down in wicker chair and patted my knee. 'Come on, Christian, be a good boy for Daddy.'

While he talked, I slowly worked the push button hotel phone off the cradle and dialed 911. I hung up as soon as I heard it answered, knowing that they would trace the call. I just needed to keep him busy. Blood ran down Ronnie's chest and pooled on my lap. I prayed that the medics and police arrived soon. Ronnie started to feel light and my entire my body was sticky.

'Do you think Santa could perform some Christmas miracle?' he asked. 'I never want to be sick again. Maybe he could wave a magic wand and turn me into a little boy. When I was a little kid, I never even noticed that I was sick.'

I started singing Christmas carols, listening for the sound of sirens. He snuggled in so close that I never noticed the gun until he pushed it against my crotch and fired. 'Merry Christmas, Daddy,' he said.

THE FÜRST NOEL
by Edward Beat

Noel discovered Jilly was a psychopath when she skewered him with a javelin at the school gymkhana.

'I am not buying her a Christmas present,' he said, his broken words drowning in scattered pools of phlegm. It had been a while since he had last spoken. He and Jemma were standing on the footpath outside Jarrods, two unanchored buoys floating on the sea of bargain-hunting humanity.

'Why not?' a grey-suited Jemma demanded. Unlike Noel, she had to be back in the office in an hour and wanted to finish her yuletide chores before the last minute rush. 'I happen to know Jilly's stolen you a very nice fake Rolex and some of Mr Wilson's best socks from his washing line. And you know what would happen to her if she's picked up again. There are only so many last chances the courts will give someone.'

Noel grunted, his voice still giving him trouble. Since he left work, he didn't get out much. Actually the Rolex was a big deal and he needed a new watch. The socks on the other foot...

'Be nice,' Jemma continued. 'One of you has to be mature about this and it's going to have to be you.'

'She did kill me,' Noel protested.

'I know, dear. But you got better.'

Jemma and Noel had an agreement not to say murder in relation to Jilly's unfortunate aim. After all, Noel was her PE teacher on the afternoon of the fateful javelin throw. And he was dating her sister. Besides, it was a good, strong throw. Just a little wayward in direction. Instead of landing somewhere out on the poorly mown greens of St Caspian's second oval, the javelin ended up turning Noel into an inedible human shish kebab. Since finding a seven foot wooden pole sticking out of his stomach, Noel found it hard to think of an appropriate present for Jemma's criminally-inclined sister.

It was around the time of the javelin mishap Noel discovered Jemma was a voodoo princess. Which explained why he woke up the next morning with extensive stitches and a tendency to limp. Jemma had spent far too many hours training him to her standards to let death stand in the way of their relationship.

She daintily raised her arm, her blonde hair flickering like paper ribbons tied to a tornado fan, and glanced at her watch. 'I now have forty-five minutes to buy something for Jilly, mum, dad, Uncle Henry and Jasper. Are you going to waste more time or simply give in and do things my way?'

Noel shrugged and shambled towards the waiting jaws of Jarrod's sliding doors, quietly noticing his name wasn't on her list. Still, Jemma had given him the greatest gift of all, herself, and he always loved unwrapping her charcoal grey suit coat and the starched white blouse beneath.

Perhaps I should explain some things before going any further. Noel wasn't your ordinary zombie. A vegetarian ex-PE teacher, he'd been upgraded. Zombie 2.0 you might say. Losing his life but keeping his moral gastronomic principles. Sure, his blood didn't pump and he relied heavily on the power of preserving fluids instead of soap. But his flesh hadn't started to rot, and probably wouldn't for decades. He maintained a mystical ability to make bits of his body, ones that according to all science and reason should not work, continue to function normally. In fact better than normal now they were completely under his control. Noel was a zombie fürst, a prince among the undead shamblers.

Who was currently trying to decide between Rainbow Dash, Pinky Pie or a side dish of mass homicide as he experienced the slowest three-quarters of an hour since his death.

The Christmas tree stabbed the air like a 2-ply PVC arrowhead. Strands of 19 gauge wire held an assortment of plastic baubles and fabric angels aloft, preventing them from taking a kamikaze leap to the floor and the waiting claws of Ninja Kitty. A potpourri of poorly wrapped presents lay scattered beneath the fake green tips, creating a walled bed for the cat. The choral singers of the H.P Lovecraft Historical Society crooned *Mi-Go We have Heard on High* in the background while jingle bells tingled the coming of midnight on Christmas Eve, the traditional present opening time for the undead.

Noel sat in his favourite armchair with Jemma perched on the armrest, draping her head on his shoulder. Jilly, dressed in skintight leggings and a ski jacket, gleefully grabbed gifts from Ninja Kitty's razors and distributed them to the group. It was almost a perfect moment. Noel silently pledged to return Mr Wilson's socks the next morning. He didn't really like argyle anyway. But he was proud of his gifts. Except for Jilly's. He never knew what to get her. A silver, anatomically correct heart necklace, lined with ruby blood drops, hung from Jemma's neck but Jilly had thrown her copy of William Mitchell's *'How to Survive Prison for the First Time Inmate'* into the cat's litter tray as soon as she unwrapped it. She didn't even bother to flick through the pages pretending to speed read it. Maybe practical wasn't the way to go this year. The CD randomly jumped to *Do You Fear What I Fear* when a red bulb on the string of lights strangling the tree blinked into darkness, quickly followed by the rest of them.

And I appeared.

Unfortunately, in the darkness, no-one noticed.

'Ho, ho, ho,' I boomed. My red-suited belly wobbled like a jumping castle full of sumo wrestlers. They ignored me. Deliberately this time.

'Ho, ho, ho,' I chortled again, my voice reverberating with the joy of the season. Noel groaned. 'What do you want, Edward?'

Some background might be needed here. Despite the fake beard and pillow-stuffed suit, I'm not actually Santa Claus. The real Santa always puts his back out doing the normal run and rather than skip Christmas for the supernatural world, the Grimm Council asked me if I would step in this year. That's what I do. Step-in. Technically, following an unfortunate run-in with a sawn-off shotgun, I'm a ghost. After haunting the pathetic locations of my childhood grew tiring, I took out an equal opportunity case against the Council and became the first Fairy Godfather. Which is how I met Noel. Given the first time they gave me a human child to watch I almost destroyed the world, the Council decided to leave me looking after the supernatural realm under the auspices of the Dead See.

'What are you doing here, Edward? It's Christmas.' It was good see Noel again after our adventures last year when he became the zombie first minister, the right hand of death. Truly. He'd even taught the horde to play tunnel ball. A key person in quelling the Black Monday zombie riots, Noel was one of the only people who had any influence over the zombie emperor. 'What has Bob done now?'

I could never hide anything from Noel and there was only reason I would show up and wreck his Christmas celebrations. Bob, or Robert the Spruce, was the one true emperor of zombiekind. Based underground, hiding in the sewers, drains and tunnels of the world, zombies were more plentiful than anyone thought.

'He's demanded a tribute of 14,000 brains by New Year's Eve or else he says the zombie empire will collapse,' I said, playing with a foam Rudolph from the tree whose nose was blinking obscene messages in morse code. 'Something about a Global Encephalous Crisis. The world's think tanks are on the verge of collapse following yet another heads fund scandal.'

Jemma dropped her punch. 'He wants to kill 14,000 people? At Christmas?'

I nodded.

'Or?' Noel stiffened in his chair. 'There must be something we can do or you wouldn't be here.'

'Well...' I paused, dreading what was coming next. Jemma perched forward, waiting to leap into action like a female Bruce Willis near a stalling helicopter. I liked Jemma. She still thought the world was worth saving and that she could do something about it. I didn't want to break that. Especially at Christmas. 'Bob's not fundamentally a bad man. He's just lonely. And no-one should be lonely at Christmas.' Just ask television. Or Hollywood.

'But what does he want?' The armchair seemed to expand to swallow Noel as he leant back.

I looked around the room and let my gaze fall on Jilly as she tied a tinsel headband around Ninja Kitty's ears. 'A wife.'

We moved to the kitchen because that is where these conversations always take place. The aroma of freshly percolated coffee punched the air. Given he no longer drank anything, Noel brewed a powerful expresso so he could relive the memories through the scent. Jilly had stormed out, a black cloud of youthful impertinence. As she headed for the front door, trailed closely by Ninja Kitty looking to escape for a forbidden evening excursion, she screamed something about not being a bag of beans to be bartered.

Jemma sipped on her coffee, raising and lowering her 'witch' mug in an almost waltz-like tempo. 'Why Jilly?'

'Bob thinks she's got spunk.'

'Not his,' Noel muttered, earning himself a glare to outdo Medusa.

'She's only sixteen. She can't be married.'

Technically she could. The Dead See operated under the laws of fairytales, myths and legends. It was the rule of lore, not law. Age didn't matter. Only the power of the plot and this was one of the classics. 'The Council have no power to coerce the mundane world. That's why they use agents like me.'

And Noel.

'I was her teacher,' he sighed. 'She's my de-facto sister-in-law. I can't just give her to Bob like a pet.' Absentmindedly he started to refill the kettle, forgetting only Jemma was drinking.

It might have been the coffee but Jemma's hand vibrated as she thunked the mug on the table, a brown ring of concern forming where it landed. I knew what she was thinking. The good of the many versus the good of the one. Fourteen thousand deaths against one marriage. Robert wouldn't even kill her. Not until her looks started to fade and she begged him to preserve her before she succumbed to the withering of age and custom.

Fourteen thousand people.

Her sister.

No choice.

One of the great advantages of being dead is you are freed from the constraining chains of linear time. As a ghost, I had long since learned to walk my own timeline. So, while I was in the kitchen with Noel and Jemma, future me was also following Jilly. Don't bother thinking about it. It makes sense in a timey-wimey way.

After pickpocketing a wallet from a guy who should have been home hours ago, she bought herself a box of mixed doughnuts and some carbonated caffeine from a local 24-hour service station. She thought the carrot-toped guy behind the counter was cute. Jilly had a weakness for bad boys and gingers, so she often called in late at night. But she never stole from there so after some overt flirting she headed back into the cold night.

The ancient yawn of a rusty gate greeted her as she entered the nearby cemetery. Draping a plaid cloth with a rubber base on the unkept ground, she sat among the graves and munched on a strawberry iced doughnut. A lichen-covered shard of broken masonry flew through my forehead as I walked over and sat next to her.

'I'm a ghost,' I said softly. 'Sticks and stones won't break my bones because they're ashes in a jar on my parents' mantlepiece.'

She sniffed and said nothing, intently studying the random pattern of the sprinkles on her doughnut. I couldn't blame her.

'He's going to fight for you, you know?' I asked, fairly sure she didn't.

'What do you mean? Who is going to fight for me?'

'Noel.'

In his infinite wisdom, Noel had challenged Robert to a duel to save Jilly from marriage. And it did. If Noel won, he would become the zombie emperor, replacing Bob in the number one position. If he lost, under the rules of privilege, Jilly would still be freed in recognition of Noel's great sacrifice. Whatever happened she was safe. It was exactly the kind of stupid gesture the Council had ordered me to prevent. After all the recent upheaval they wanted some stability in the world of zombie affairs.

'Why?' It was a quiet whisper, as much to the nearest headstone as to me.

I didn't know. She was, after all, the person who deliberately threw a javelin through his stomach because she didn't care if she flunked PE. Noel was just one of those people. He'd even befriended a failed ghost who fought to become a fairy godfather in a futile search for meaning.

'Why not?'

I shrugged. It was the best answer I could give. A blanket of grey, soot-stained snow slushed from the sky, draping us in a cold blanket. Overhead, there was no Christmas star, no miracle. Jilly chewed on her doughnuts. The memory, the ghost, of the wind grabbed my fake beard seconds after it passed in real life. Since I died, I was always a few seconds too late. Haunted by the memories of completed touches, the aftertaste of flavours and the echoes of sounds, trapped in a world of the past.

A ghost of Christmas yesterday yearning for tomorrows destined to never come. But tonight, tonight of all nights, I was also Santa Claus. Summoning my big red fur-lined bag, I reached into its cavernous mouth and wished. And hoped.

'Merry Christmas,' I said, handing the small package to Jilly who tore furiously at the silver wrapping.

It was a director's cut of Romero's *Dawn of the Dead*. And a paper printout from Wiccapedia.

In colour. Colour was important.

Zombie duels are not to the death. That would be crazy. And pointless. As crazy as writing these stories via ouija board. But you don't want to hear about my problems. Zombie duels are to the life. Which was particularly hard for Noel as a vegetarian. Each zombie would absorb the vitality, the deathforce, of the other until one consumed so much they were restored to life. The living perosn was the loser. The other remained a zombie and therefore won. Their prize was to eat the loser and thus reabsorb their lost vitality as well as the essence of the vanquished. Even if he won and remained a zombie, Noel wasn't keen on the idea of eating Bob.

Almost religious events, duels were held in the Croft. One of the few aboveground places zombies congregated except to eat, the grassy meadow was a kind of church au naturale for zombiekind.

'Are you sure you want to go through with this?'

Surrounded by a horde of zombies worse than any football hooligans, Noel nodded. The last duel fought here was when Robert replaced Markus as emperor, a duel Noel and I helped him win. They were seated at a stone table, but this one wasn't waiting to broken by a lion's death. Despite my status as a representative of the Grimm Council, I had handed the officiating duties over to my yuletide offsider, the horned incubus Krampus. Glad to be raised from his henchman status, Krampie made sure everything was being done according to the lore.

'Any last words?' Robert asked, his crevassed skin showing the decades of his death. He looked like a traditional zombie, decayed and stained with the strain of undead centuries.

Noel just shrugged. 'We're zombies. Not vampires and werewolves. We don't talk out our problems across an empty field.'

A rope of hazy green light spewed from the mouths of the two opponents, wrapping itself around the other's throat. You could barely hear a Angelo Badalamenti jazz guitar as the assembled zombie horde watched, fascinated, in the dawning light. Lines of pain and concentration etched themselves on Noel's forehead. He looked at Jemma, a death of love and longing burned into the emerald noose around his neck.

The air around Robert shimmered with sheer power, as if he were made of overheated metal, warping his aura. And smiled. Noel's skin faded like microwaved parchment. He was starting to glow, his body being to revert to life.

'For your presumption in challenging, you have earned no privilege. I will have your life. And, then, I will have a wife. And then my tribute. Today, I have bought my throne with blood.'

It was Christmas morning. I was the supernatural Santa Claus and I had nothing in my gift bag. Not even Krampus could help. There wasn't room in his coal bag for Robert. I glanced at Jemma who was mouthing the words of a spell I suspect was designed to boost Noel's vitality. Pointlessly. No external magic could affect the participants of a zombie duel. It all came down to the duelists and what power they had inside.

Unless.

A wild idea struck me.

Noel's eyelids flickered and his head slumped towards the table. His zombie vitality at empty, his body moments away from hitting the reboot key into life. Something he had desired since he first died. But not like this. This was not the Christmas miracle he had prayed for, not a dream wrapped in Jemma's arms. Robert's grin opened and a white flood of drool burst the embankment of his lips.

I was a ghost. Not Santa. Not a fairy godfather. A ghost. So I dived in and possessed Noel's body.

The explosion of centuries of pent-up death shattered the link between the two duelists. My ties to the world, the hooked chains binding me to this mortal coil, were more powerful than any zombie magic. They might be the living dead. I was dead. Period. No flesh. No physical body. As a ghost, I was pure death, vitality incarnate.

And I was merged with Noel. Internal, not external.

All according to the lore.

Noel opened his eyes as I left his body. 'I'm still dead.' His head jerked from side to side, testing the reality of his ongoing deceased status. Krampus was patting him on the back like a friend congratulating a new father. He wasn't just still dead, he was the new zombie emperor. Noel the First.

Instead of an aged carcass of a man, a red-haired teenager with a pulse sat in Robert's place. Taking his first breaths in more than a hundred years, Robert watched a mist of dragonbreath condense in the morning cool.

I'd done it. I'd saved the day.

Than the chant started.

'Eat. Eat. Eat,' the gathered zombies cried.

Noel hesitated.

'No, I'll take him,' screamed Jilly, appearing on the scene with perfect timing thanks to future me. 'I'll even marry him if you want. Just don't kill him. He's cute.'

The Wiccapedia printout detailing Robert's criminal past before being zombified poked from the back pockets of her jeans. The photo of a carrot-topped athlete with the body of a movie star. It was a match made in, well, the unredeeming pits of purgatory actually.

Confused, Noel opened and shut his mouth as if eating the air instead of Robert.

'Make him your coronation gift to her,' I whispered to the befuddled Noel. It was allowed under the largess of new emperor. Jemma wiped a tear from her eye. At last he'd found the perfect present for her sister.

He looked at Jilly and Robert cuddling like the teenagers they now were and nodded. 'Merry Christmas,' he said.

A VISIT FROM SANTA
by David Williamson

The instant his eyes were open, the small boy kicked off his bedclothes and leapt from his bed, podgy little feet stepping automatically into his Sponge Bob slippers. He tugged his dressing gown from the hook behind his bedroom door and was still pulling it on as he headed downstairs.

It was almost *the* day!

Now he could at last open his final window... after twenty three days of seemingly endless waiting. Then, he would wake up tomorrow morning and... *yippee*!

'What on earth are you doing up at *this* hour, Toby?' his mother was sitting at the kitchen table, sipping at her first coffee of the day and relishing the peace and quiet before the hectic business of food shopping began. She knew full well the reason for Toby being up so early, and smiled to herself, remembering her own excitement when she'd been his age.

She took Toby's tiny six year old hand and steered him over to the larder, where she had pinned his advent calendar, twenty four days earlier. His small fingers flexed in anticipation as his eyes scanned for the last remaining door.

'You know which number to open?' she asked, needlessly, as he was already attacking the tiny cardboard portal with trembling hands.

'Ah... it's baby Jesus in the manger!' he said, before stuffing the small chocolate treat into his mouth. He stood looking both awestruck at the small picture, and slightly disappointed that he had eaten his last chocolate from the calendar.

Jane knew that it would be a very long day ahead, and not only because of her impending battle at the supermarket, which she recalled from past experience, would be heaving with Christmas Eve shoppers.

She also realised that Toby would take a lot of persuading to get him to bed that evening, and then he'd be listening on the landing for half the night, waiting for Santa to call.

Not to mention the certainty that he'd be up way before dawn had cracked, making one hell of a racket as he tore open his presents and oohed and aahed over them until she was forced to get out of bed and go and join him downstairs!

But that was all part of the joy of Christmas... or so everyone kept telling her. No personal pleasure for her of course, but Toby would be happy... for a change.

The six years old's expression suddenly clouded over and his bottom lip began to tremble. Jane knew what was coming and immediately tried to steer his thoughts in another direction.

'What would you like for breakfast, darling?' she asked, hopefully.

But it was already too late.

'Mummy... ' he said as though she hadn't spoken, 'I wish Daddy could be here with us... ? I wish... ' and the tears erupted from his eyes, a lump in his throat stopping him from saying anything further.

Jane drew her son close and held him tight. Her heart ached for her son's sadness, and she knew that she could never get him what he really wanted for Christmas... his Father.

She ruffled the boy's hair 'Come on, Toby... you know that Daddy can't come back to us? It's been two years now since he was taken from us... I'd like him to be here too, but... well... that's just the way things are... sorry, darling... '

The two of them sat huddled on the sofa, hugging one another and crying softly. A young boy and his mother, alone in the world and fending for themselves as best they could.

Still... whatever happened, it simply *had* to be better than that Christmas of two years ago... ?

It was well past nine in the evening when Jane finally persuaded the tired and more than a little ratty Toby to get into his bed.

'But I'll miss Santa and Rudolph! ' he'd wailed.

Jane was almost at the end of her tether, and a smart slap to the bottom would be the next thing on offer as all reasoning had failed, when the doorbell rang.

'It's *him*... he's *here!*' Toby leapt down the stairs, two at a time and he was half way to the front door before Jane managed to pull him up short.

'Just you stop where you are, young man! ' she shouted, angrily, 'I'm the only person who answers the door at this time of night! ' and she steered her son into the lounge, before closing the door firmly behind him.

Jane heard Toby wailing in protest as she checked herself in the mirror, smoothing her plain white dress over her hips and fluffing her hair.

The bell rang impatiently once more, and she flicked on the porch light and opened the door.

There were two police officers standing there, a Sergeant and a young WPC, but the look on their faces worried her immediately. They glanced at one another, before the sergeant spoke.

'Mrs. Roberts... ?' he asked, politely.

Jane nodded dumbly, pulling the door slightly to, in case Toby decided to listen in.

Ten minutes later, she walked back into the lounge, her face pale and drawn looking, deep worry lines etched across her brow. Thank God, the boy had fallen asleep on the hearth rug in front of the fire, thumb crammed into his small mouth, tears of anger and frustration drying on his cheeks and his favourite teddy tucked beneath one arm.

He woke up as Jane hoisted him up from the rug, and he looked at her as though he didn't know who she was, briefly.

'Was it Santa, Mummy?' he asked, sleepily.

Jane broke into a nervous smile and shook her head.

'No, darling... only carol singers. Come on Mr. Sleepyhead... it's bed for you.'

They were just outside of his bedroom door, when Toby suddenly tried to wriggle free from his mother's grip.

'What on earth are you doing, Toby?' she snapped, gripping onto the banister rail for support as he squirmed about.

'Mummy! Did you put the mince pie and the whiskey out for him? ' he asked, eyes bright with concern.

Jane sighed, but then smiled. 'Not yet... but the sooner you get into bed, the sooner I can do it! ' and with that, he popped into his bed without further comment, and was asleep as his head hit the pillow.

It was still very dark outside when he awoke. His nightlight shone from its place on top of the chest of drawers, lighting up his teddies and books on the wall shelves beside his bed. Everything was quiet outside, so he knew it must be very early, and that his mother would still be fast asleep in her room next door. She gone to bed really late and he had heard her brushing her teeth before closing her bedroom door.

He had also heard her crying softly, just as she had done when Daddy had been taken from them, all that time ago.

He didn't like to hear her weeping like that, it made him feel sad, but there was nothing he could do to make her feel better... he wished that there were.

But now he had to check something... it had been worrying him since he'd gone to bed.

Toby pushed back his covers and tiptoed over to his bedroom door. When he was satisfied that his mother was asleep, he tip-toed quietly down the stairs, opened the lounge door and crept inside. He smiled as he noticed the whiskey and mince pie on the coffee table, just as Mummy had promised. He had one more thing to do and then, satisfied, he made his way silently back to his room and the warmth of his bed.

He awoke several hours later, to the faint sound of a gentle tapping against his bedroom window, and leapt out to investigate.

'Wow... *snow!*' he yelled, pressing his nose up against the cold glass, his breath condensing upon its surface. He *really* wanted to rush in and tell Mummy, but it was still quiet downstairs, so he guessed she was having a lie-in and decided to leave her in peace... for a while.

Then he remembered: his presents! How *could* he have forgotten those?

He galloped down the stairs with no attempt at stealth this time, and burst through the lounge door, grinning from ear to ear at the large pile of Christmas presents, all wrapped in a bright red paper and stacked under the tree.

He was half way through tearing open his first present, when the man spoke to him. 'Hello, Toby... have you missed me, son? '

The boy stopped in mid-rip, his tiny mouth gaped open and he swung around so quickly, that he lost his balance and fell to his knees. Could it *really* be? No... God had taken him away... *Mummy* said!

'What's the matter, son... don't you recognise me? Didn't you want to see your old Dad at Christmas time?' asked the man, sitting in the large chair beside the fireplace... Daddy's chair.

The six year old licked his lips nervously and got to his feet, then stepped back a pace, uncertain what to say or do next. The man held out his arms and beckoned the boy to him, but Toby stood his ground, and eyed the man suspiciously.

It was all so long ago, to his young mind at least... the memory so vague. After all, he had only been four when his father had been taken from them? This man *could* be his Daddy... he did look a bit like him..?

'You don't have much to say to your Daddy after so long, do you? And after all the trouble I've taken to come and visit you and Mummy? '

The man smiled and produced a package from the side of his chair.'Look... I've even brought you a present, son,' and he raised the gift aloft for Toby to get a better view. The boy automatically took a step forward, then checked himself. He was wary of this man, but had no idea why. After all, hadn't he been praying to God all those nights for Daddy to come back to them... ?

A distant, fleeting memory stirred in the back of his mind, and he frowned as he tried to recall what it was. But the bright red present *did* look very tempting to the six year old. He really wanted to know what it was, but his legs refused to move for some reason.

'Aah... don't be shy, Toby... here, I'll roll it over to you and you can open it there, if you like? '

The boy was torn between the promise of the present and the strange look in the man's eyes. He was smiling, but he didn't look *right* somehow.

Toby nodded, and stayed where he was. Did the man/his Daddy say 'roll'? It must be a new football then... wow! The man pulled back his arm and let go of the ball, but it didn't roll very well and came to rest half way between where he sat in his chair and Toby, over near the Christmas tree.

For a moment, they both stared at the present, but the Toby's curiosity had reached bursting point, and he scurried across the room, snatched up the present and then sat cross legged on the carpet. His hands were shaking with excitement as he tore off the wrapping.

His father stood up from the fireside chair.

Toby stared at the present with a puzzled expression for a moment.

Why had Daddy bought him a make-up doll for Christmas?

The boy hardly noticed the man laughing. A horrible, insane, laugh which came from deep inside the man's chest and seemed to boom around the walls of the quiet lounge. Toby finally worked out what it was he was holding in his hands, and dropped in onto the floor. He tried to scream, but he was too horrified and his throat seemed to close up.

His Mummy's severed head, still partially wrapped in bright Christmas paper, stared back at him from the carpet.

His Daddy stood over him, gently stroking the razor sharp edge of the carving knife which he had taken from the kitchen drawer the night before.

It was nice of someone to leave the patio doors unlocked for him. Presumably, that had been Toby's idea so that Santa could get in to leave the presents, as they didn't have a chimney?

Jane had been asleep in bed, the bitch, and she had died without ever waking when he had sliced her throat.

Toby looked up at the man.

He remembered now... it *was* his Daddy... he knew that now.

He recognised the insane look in his eyes, the same look he had seen two years ago on this very day, when he had murdered Toby's elder sister for making too much noise with her new wind up puppy.

That was when his father had been 'taken' from them, dragged away, screaming and hysterical by armed police, but not before slashing Jane's cheek and knifing one of the officers.

Toby recalled it all now, every detail of the terrible memory he had blocked from his young mind.

And he finally found the strength to scream, briefly, before the madman, his Daddy, dragged the boy up by his hair and slit his throat, just as the first desperate knocks of the police started pounding at the front door....

PRANCER'S STORY
by UZ Eliserio

Crazy? I guess you could call him that. For me, it was more about following policy. Ever since he was twelve, that kid had been nice. As in real nice, not just makes-his-own bed nice, or doesn't-kick-cats nice, as in, helped-build-the-town-well nice, cooks-for-his-mother-who-has-two-jobs-nice, like I said, real nice. And this was on his twelfth year!

So, Santa waited for Jimmy's letter. After all, no kid is that nice for the sake of niceness. Santa knew Jimmy wanted something special for Christmas. But the morning of December 24 came and Jimmy's letter was nowhere to be found. Santa was so nervous! He took half of the elves from toy-making duty and had them searching the factories, the barracks, even the nearby hills. And when they couldn't find it, he went to the post office to complain. He took me with him, because it was still light and I was the fastest flyer. The Post Master General told us Jimmy didn't send Santa a letter. The nice kid, it seemed then, was being nice for the sake of being nice. Or, in any case, not for a gift.

This went on for four more years. Each year, Jimmy helped at the orphanage, studied hard, performed at the school plays. He's a real good actor, that one. Each year, Santa waited for Jimmy's letter. Each year, Jimmy's letter failed to arrive.

Santa was biting his fingers all December of Jimmy's seventeenth year. Once he turned eighteen, he was no longer a kid, Santa couldn't give him a present anymore. He was going to turn eighteen on January. 'Surely,' Santa told me, 'he's been good, perfectly good, for five years now, surely he wants something.'

He tightened his grip on my antlers. 'I'll get him anything! All he needs to do is ask!'

As it turned out, Jimmy sent a letter that year. It arrived on December first. Jimmy asked for one thing. A nanobot creator. 'I know,' he wrote, 'that you're the only one who could give me this gift. And I know you'll do whatever you can so I can have it for Christmas.'

This time Santa took all the elves off their current work. 'Make that toy!'

'It's not a toy, Santa,' I said, 'It's a machine that makes really tiny robots.'

He pulled at his beard. 'Well then,' he told the elves, 'make that machine!'

The elves worked all day and all night, up to December 23. They just didn't have the know-how and scientific knowledge to make a nanobot creator.

'I failed him,' Santa said, 'he was the nicest kid ever, and I couldn't give him what he wanted for Christmas.' He sat down on the snow and wept. 'If my son were alive, you know, he'd be Jimmy's age. Ah,' he hit his fist on the ground, 'no, wait. Jimmy's one year older.'

I was moved by pity. I guess that's why I researched Jimmy's gift on the Internet weeks before. This was when I became part of the problem. I told Santa that there was a nanobot creator at Area 51.

'Area 51!' he said, standing up suddenly, stepping on my hoof. 'That's just a few miles away from here!'

We left the North Pole immediately.

Area 51 was a gigantic warehouse. Its walls were made of glass, to obscure it from any outsider's view. So sure were they of this security measure that there was only one soldier standing guard. Santa couldn't see it until I made him look at it from an angle. 'It shimmers,' he said, 'like air from a boiling pot.'

'Air does not shimmer,' I said.

'Quiet.' He reached into his bag of toys, spilling out more than a dozen wind up dolls. 'This should distract him for a while.' He kicked some of them towards me. 'Help would be appreciated.'

'If I told you once, I've told you a million times, hooves are not hands.'

He smirked and wound up the dolls. 'You only tell me that when it's convenient for you.'

One by one he sent them at the warehouse, like an army marching on enemy territory. It worked. The soldier followed the dolls as they passed Area 51 on the way to nowhere. Santa was fat, and my hooves made quite a racket, but we got in without any alarms being raised.

Inside were boxes piled upon boxes, sitting neatly side by side on mile long shelves. 'Where is it?' Santa asked.

'Wait.' I checked my tablet. 'Grid 16, lot 41.'

It took us some time, trying to find it. There were so many distractions. Talking skulls, glowing chests, self-playing guitars. I almost got sucked in by a portable wormhole. Santa pulled me out. He was feverish in his desire to get Jimmy that nanobot creator. It was this desire that finally led us to it.

'There,' he said, pointing at a small box on the top shelf. 'Lot 41.'

'Get on, then,' I said, offering my back. I floated up. 'Got it?'

'Got it!'

'Halt! You, in the red shirt!'

I didn't wait for Santa's command. I flew straight for the walls. 'Close your eyes!' I shouted. I closed my eyes and rammed the glass, my antlers leading the charge.

Santa laughed all the way back to the North Pole. Safe at last, he had the elves take care of me. 'You don't have to ride out tomorrow night,' he said. 'I'll be at my office.'

'Wait,' I said to his back. 'Let me see it.'

'What?' He looked at me with his thick white eyebrows raised. 'See what? Oh.' He looked at the box. He looked at the elves. He waited for them to finish bandaging my antlers and forelegs, then he dismissed them. Even when they were gone, though, he wasn't satisfied. Even then he was paranoid. 'Come, let's do this in my office.' He walked away.

I followed him. I had to wipe my hooves two times on his welcome mat before he let me through the door. Even then he was obsessive compulsive. 'Well, open it.'

He set the box on his table. 'Here it is. The toy for the nicest boy in the world.'

'It's not a toy.' It looked like an anthill, with a tablet attached to one side. I was about to type something but Santa slapped my hoof away.

'Don't touch it. It's Jimmy's.'

I sighed. 'Bit of an anticlimax, if you ask me.' I stepped out of the office, went to my sleeping quarters at the stables. I took the next three days off. The elves were busy manufacturing last minute wishes, the reindeer were tired from flying all over the world, the snow was terribly cruel and cold, but I just lay there and enjoyed myself, surfing the Internet.

It was December 28 when I decided I needed to stretch my legs a bit. My wounds had healed, so I flew around the factory grounds. It was from a height of 10,000 miles that I saw Santa, punching a snowman. I landed quietly a few feet behind him.

'Stupid, stupid,' he said, crushing a charcoal and carrot in his hands. 'How could I have been tricked like this?'

'Tricked? By whom?'

He turned around, saw me, charged at me. 'You! Were you a part of this?'

I realized he was going to grab my antlers, so I floated up a few feet. 'Part of what?' His eyes were red, blazing anger. 'Have you gone insane?'

'Ah, watch the news.' He stalked away.

'Hey,' I shouted at this back, 'I read have an RSS feed of the *Guardian*. They have news!'

I asked around.

Rudolph looked at me like I had a red nose. 'The Elf Channel,' was the only thing he said.

I guess Santa's mood infected everyone. Usually we were all very happy the days following Christmas. I tuned in to the Elf Channel. It was the top headline. Jimmy Montreal had taken over Sambalon Town.

The details were easy enough to follow. Using his army of nanobots, Jimmy poisoned the town well, taking over people's minds. Taking over, he had them raise mile high walls, to protect against foreigners and other undesirables. The Elf Channel showed renegade footage of people starving, dissidents in prison. Apparently, statistically there always had to be a percentage of a population immune to diseases, even ones as complicated as nanobots.

I fell to my knees. This was my fault. I found the machine, I helped Santa break into Area 51. I too had made this kid into a dictator.

Santa couldn't touch him, not until next Christmas anyway, and by that time he wouldn't be a kid anymore. Naughty or nice, he would be out of Santa's purview. So I had to be the one to stop him. I had to be the one to put things right.

I went to the one thing that solved all of my problems, the Internet. I researched all I could about Jimmy Montreal. I used Google, Bing, Yahoo, Duckduckgo. I found out all his forum aliases. I paid all kinds of shady people to hack into his email and social media accounts. For months I was at the computer day and night. My eyes bled. The elves kept joking that they needed a red mouthed reindeer next, given that they already had a red nosed and red eyed one.

One day mid-July the elves told me I was the only reindeer left. Rudolph, they said, flew away early in the morning.

It was from the elves too that I found out how bad Santa took the con. He was always drinking, they said. His belly size had doubled. He didn't trim his beard anymore, it reached down to his waist, the elves said. 'And he keeps writing Jimmy's name,' they said, 'like he's trying to curse him or something.'

'Keep him alive,' I told them. 'I'm close to finding out what we need.' I hit the jackpot late November. It's amazing what a reindeer could find out about someone with just their full name and a sample of their handwriting.

Jimmy, it turned out, was Santa's son. But that wasn't the interesting part. He had lied about how old he was. He wasn't turning eighteen in January. He was turning seventeen. Based on the one picture I found of him, he didn't look his age. He was still a boy, his face was fresh, except for a pus-filled pimple on the lower right of his forehead. His hair was close cropped, neat, and he was grinning. Happy. He wasn't going to be happy soon. His age meant that Santa could go after him that December. It meant I wasn't alone in my revenge.

I went to Santa immediately. I found out that the elves were lying. Santa wasn't just in a bad shape. Yeah, I admit it now. He's crazy.

I found him in his office, surrounded by bottles. He wasn't even drinking, he was just pouring the beer on his face. There were rats poking out of his beard. It was a nest of pests, home too to cockroaches and flies. His belly wasn't big, it was bulging, with several unnatural bumps. He still laughed, though. A sad, desperate laugh. Like he was sucking me in.

He spoke first. 'He's my son,' he said.

There was no computer in Santa's office. 'Did the elves tell you?'

He shook his head, sending a spider climbing his face down the floor. 'I named him Jimmy. I racked my brains, thinking if I ever met a woman with the last name Montreal.' He threw a bottle of beer at me. I caught it with my antlers and hooves. 'I didn't, but I did date one from Montreal.' He laughed. I dropped the bottle.

'He's not eighteen, you know.'

He was about to pour another bottle of beer down his face. He stopped midway, pouring the beer down his chest. 'What?'

'You can still get him. You and I, we can get him.'

'He lied about his age? That's even worse than using the nanobots against the people of his town.' He struggled to get up, staggering on his feet. 'Let's go. Let's go get him.'

'Don't we have to wait until Christmas?'

'He lied about his age. His gift is forfeit. We have to take the nanobot creator back.' He looked at me straight in the eye, sniffing. 'The others, they left.'

It wasn't a question, so I didn't answer.

'An aerial bombardment's out of the question, then. Never mind, I have a backup plan.' He smashed a bottle of beer against the wall. He held on tight to the neck of his just-made weapon. 'There's a portal, in their well. We'll go through that.'

'How do you know about this?'

'I've been planning an assault at Sambalon for six months now,' he said, kicking the door open.

'But you didn't know he wasn't a kid anymore. Isn't that a violation of policy?'

He flexed his muscles. 'Don't tell anyone.'

Besides the elves, who could I tell? And most probably, the elves already knew about it. Which meant that they've already told everyone. It didn't matter that Santa *had* planned to violate policy. What mattered was, what we were going to do *was* according to policy. And there's nothing better than beating up a seventeen year old in accordance with the law.

Fittingly enough, the hole through which we had to go to land at the bottom of Sambalon's well was located at Area 51. Because of our raid months before, they beefed up their security. But Santa and I were determined. The factories were breaking down, the other reindeer had abandoned us, the elves did nothing but gossip. We needed this revenge. We were going to get it.

There were guards all over the perimeter. On top of the glass building was a massive camera, the shape of an eye, spinning like a coin, watching for intruders. We talked strategy on the top of a mountain overlooking Area 51. We built and hid behind a family of snowmen.

'I say we call the elves,' Santa said, 'send them on a raid to provide a distraction.' They were close by, we knew we would need back up.

'How about we gather all the remaining toys and use those to bribe the guards?' I thought my plan was good, but he shot it down with a raised eyebrow.

'Let's just hop on the sleigh and ram through their defenses.' He packed a snowball in his bare hands, the mice had taken off with his red mittens, and threw it at me.

'Quit it!'

He hit me with another one.

'Hey, there can be rocks in those!' I actually didn't mind this. It wasn't painful, and it was good to see him having a little fun again. He was about to throw another snowball at me but instead he lifted it up to the sun. I was afraid he'd lost his mind at that moment. Lost it, as in emptied. I knew he was mad.

'I got it,' he said, 'I know how we'll get in.' He pitched the idea, and before I could critique it he had put me on the sleigh and was on the phone calling up our back-up elves. They were only a few miles away, and arrived with Santa and me belly deep in snow. 'Come on, you guys,' he said, 'finish the job.'

They finished the job, all right. They even whistled while they worked, not even bothering to hide the fact that they loved burying me. It was cold inside, and large as the ball had become, my antlers still stuck out. 'How will we know if they pushed us already?'

The world tumbled down, and the answer to my question came as Santa's vomit.

The ball exploded when we hit Area 51's glass wall. Our attack knocked down the shelves, sending boxes of alien lifeform and Victorian-era weaponry flying. I dragged Santa out of the snow, seeing in the corner of my eye that we had flattened more than a few of the soldiers standing guard. 'Where's the hole? Where's the hole?'

'Grid 12, lot 12.'

I found it, tossed him in. A laser took a bit of my antlers as I jumped to follow him in. I screamed in pain, and then I heard Santa shriek. I had landed on him. We were submerged in water. 'Swim up,' I said. 'swim up.' His back was to me. I couldn't tell if he heard anything I said. I rammed him with my antlers, and he swam up.

The snow and the water should have been enough to freeze me to death, but my heart was pumping and I felt vigorous. It was the gift of hate. Stuck there at the bottom of the well, Santa elbowing me for space, I swear I could smell Jimmy, even though I'd never actually been close enough to him to pick up his scent. 'What do we do now?'

'We wait for someone to throw down a bucket.' Santa was scrubbing his face. The snow ball ride had killed most of his beard's inhabitants. He cleaned it in the water. It was like he was trying to wash the madness from his eyes. It wasn't evident if he succeeded.

I saw my reflection. I saw that we shared a look. 'Hey, listen. When we get him, what exactly are we going to do?'

A bucket made of wood landed on Santa's head. He grinned. 'Grab on to me,' he said, gripping the rope. 'I'm going to teach this kid that Santa doesn't mean saint.'

Someone strong was pulling us up, or, more probably, several people. A bad feeling formed in my gut, the acid reaching my mouth. Did we come all this way for death? We reached the mouth of the well, and it dawned on me that we did. There were about a dozen men and women there. They had white eyes, and guns in their hands.

I recognized Jimmy at once. For one thing, his eyes were a normal black on white. For another, he carried the nanobot creator with him. And for another another, he still had that damned pus-filled pimple on his forehead. 'Welcome, Father. And you too, Mr. Reindeer.'

'The name's Prancer,' I said, steam escaping from my nose. I was getting ready to charge.

Santa slightly pulled at my tail. 'Not yet,' he whispered. To Jimmy, he said, 'Hello, son. There's no need for guns. Send your goons away, I won't hurt you.'

I glanced at him. It seemed the bath from the bottom of the well had an effect on him. His eyes were clear. And he was speaking softly, as if he were fond of the dictator of Sambalon. How exactly did he plan to teach the kid that he wasn't a saint? By proving he was a nurse? A nanny? A caregiver?

'Trust me,' he whispered again, raising his hands. 'We surrender,' he told Jimmy. 'Right, Prancer?'

I counted to ten. Licking my lips, I said, 'We surrender.'

Jimmy nodded. 'Very well.' He typed something on the nanobot creator, and all but two men stayed. 'Follow me,' he said, turning his back on us and walking towards the center of the town.

I had memorized Sambalon's geography, of course, I knew where he was taking us. 'We're heading to his house,' I told Santa. One of the men poked my ass with his gun, and I walked faster.

Santa matched my pace. 'I know. Thanks for backing up me back there.'

'Next time I won't be so trusting. Your plan better work.'

'I hope so,' he said.

'So you do have plan? What is it? Come on, tell me. Wait, what? Do you have a plan?'

He just stroked my back.

Presently, we arrived at Jimmy's house. He typed some more, and the two men stayed by the door. 'Come on in,' he told us. He went straight to the stairs, and all of us climbed to the third floor.

The wood creaked under my hooves. I caught the scent of fresh coffee. Santa's blend, I could tell. Black, no sugar, no cream, just plain good coffee. I prefer mine iced, with all the works. At the third floor we found a table full of cookies, candies, and ham. Besides the coffee there was eggnog too. There was a sofa in front of a fireplace, and at the far end was a window. A woman was there, on a rocking chair. She was knitting. Mittens, I saw. She was knitting mittens.

'Heloise?' Santa said. He went to her, and I followed him.

'Hello, Santa.' Her voice was different. Inhuman. Like she was speaking under water, each syllable was punctuated by an air bubble popping. I saw why when we got to her. Her chest had caved in. There were tiny metal creatures there, cutting off dead skin and muscles, constructing pipes, levels, and platforms. 'Goodbye, Santa.'

It was a recording. She wasn't really actually reanimated. Yet.

'She told me about you,' Jimmy said behind us, 'told me about the technology and magic at your disposal. And she taught me how to manipulate you. As I grew, I plotted revenge. You abandoned us. And then she became sick. I thought about asking you for help, but she said you were useless. Then it hit me, I could have my vengeance and save mother at the same time. Use you to steal the nanobot creator. I knew about the policy. Naughty and nice. I knew you'd come after me.' He put the machine down. He raised his fists. 'Come on. I don't need anything to take you on. Come on.' He was a kid. A stupid, evil kid.

Santa fell to his knees, hugging Heloise's legs. 'I'm sorry. Heloise, I'm sorry. Son, please forgive me.'

At that moment I knew that justice was no longer in his mind. This boy had tricked us, caused us madness, destroyed our operations at the North Pole, and there he was, on the floor, begging for forgiveness. He had no plan, I realized. Or rather, his plan was to burst in tears and beat at his chest.

'Oh, Father.' Jimmy came to him, hugging him from behind. 'Mother, Mother Father is here. Won't you say hi to him? Mother?'

They were both on their knees, worshipping the still dead woman. Jimmy's master.

'This kid,' I said, 'still has the whole village under his control.' I walked towards the nanobot creator.

'I'll let them go,' Jimmy said. 'Father, they wanted me to burn her. She died mid-November. I sent my letter as soon as she did. They wanted me to burn her, said she had some disease. Father, please. I'll let them go as soon as the nanobots are done.'

I stomped on the machine before Santa could speak.

'No!' Jimmy shouted, moving to stand up and charge me. Santa pinned him to the floor with an embrace. 'Mother! Mother no!' He wailed, slamming his fists on the floor.

I walked towards them.

'Prancer, please,' Santa said. 'He's my son. Please, understand. It's my fault. I made him turn out this way. I love him. I'll make him better. Please. Prancer, my friend. You understand, don't you? Don't you?'

I shoved him aside with my antlers, and planted my hoof on Jimmy's forehead. I broke his skull. Bits of bone and blood clung to the hair of my legs. I stomped on his face, again and again, telling Santa, 'I don't, I don't, I don't.'

THE WITHOUT MAN
by LF Robertson

It is the Winter of 1999.

December 19th: Six days 'til Christmas

'This is for you.' The object presented with the words was slim and oblong. Stylized red reindeer leapt and galloped across the surface on a field of bright, metallic blue, while shiny red ribbon entwined itself about the sides, snaking upwards to form a neat bow with scissor-curled ends that danced out beneath it.

Polly studied the proffered gift with a solemnity uncommon in most ten year olds when faced with something wrapped in colourful, crinkling paper that rustled in protest wherever there were fingers dug into it. 'It's not Christmas yet.'

'I know, but I know you were upset about not seeing mum and dad 'til Christmas Eve, and staying so long with Auntie Judith. I thought you could have this early to cheer you up a bit.'

'They should be home.' Polly insisted. 'It's nearly Christmas. Dad promised we'd go ice-skating.'

He shrugged helplessly. 'Well, they're not. Do you want to open it?'

After a pause, Polly nodded, taking the present from him and sliding one hand along the ribbon until she found a tag. On the outside, a similarly stylized Rudolph beamed out at her. On the inside, in the kind of carefully bland handwriting that suggested the writer was making a strong effort to make it as legible as possible were the words:

> *Dear Polly,*
> *Merry Christmas!*
> *Cole*
> *xox*

Having carefully prised off the tag, and its accompanying cluster of twirling ribbons, Polly showed no such consideration to the rest of the wrapping. Scrabbling fingernails worked at the sides until they found a spot to worm their way beneath, then a brief struggle ensued before it gave way, a great tear forming down the middle before Polly ripped the paper apart entirely and discarded it on the floor.

The object within was a leather-bound red book filled with thick, cream-coloured drawing-paper. Flipping the inside cover open revealed the words (in the same stock writing as before),

'Christmas Rhymes, Carols and Songs: A Selection'

Then in smaller writing underneath,

'A Christmas Collection, gathered and illustrated by Nicholas Bertram'

'I hope you like it.' Cole added, chewing the nails of his right hand as Polly flicked through the first few pages, a small smile playing on her lips.

'It's amazing. I like this one.' She turned the book around, carefully supporting it in the crook of her elbow and pointing to the illustration in question with her free hand. A mouse and a mole in neat vests and jackets worked together to deck the halls—and the page—with boughs of holly. 'Who wrote it all out? It's really neat.'

'Me.' At Polly's doubtful and mildly accusing look, Cole admitted, 'Well, I used a stencil. I thought it'd look nicer than typing it up and gluing it in.'

'It must have taken ages. Thank you.' She caught him in a one-armed hug, but was gone before he had a chance to return it. She thumbed through the pages, turning them with more care when something did catch her eye, only to pause at the end.

'I don't recognise this one.' She glanced up, doubt creeping into her voice as her brows drew together in confusion. 'Are you sure this one's about Christmas?'

'Which one?' he asked, 'All the ones I picked were about Christmas, one way or another.'

She shifted the book to get a better grip on it, and then began to read aloud in a sing-song tone, her voice ringing out clearly in the empty hallway:

> *He's come to tuck you in to bed,*
> *The man without fingers, stomach, and head,*
> *Your night-gown or shirt he'll help to lace,*
> *The man without fingers, stomach, and face,*
> #
> *But if near midnight you tip-toe down,*
> *The man without fingers, stomach, and crown*
> *Will snatch you up, and return you to bed,*
> *Without your fingers, and stomach, and head.*

Cole frowned. 'I've never even heard that before. What's it called? Does it say who it's by?'

'`The Without Man`, no name given.' A pause, then, 'I'm glad you didn't draw a picture.'

'That's really weird. I'm sure the book was blank when I bought it… But I didn't check every page, maybe it was already there?' Polly didn't look any more convinced than he felt. 'Well, I don't know, but it doesn't sound very Christmassy, and therefore, has no place in your Christmas present. I'll cut it out, if you like.'

He held his hands out to receive the book, but Polly's arms tightened about it, gaze again drawing to the poem. The silence stretched out between them, making Cole feel bizarrely uncomfortable. 'Polly?'

'Maybe it does belong.'

'What?'

'Maybe it's meant to scare children into being good. It says not to tip-toe down near midnight.' She pointed to the relevant part, but Cole found himself with little desire to step closer and look. 'That's when Santa comes. Santa brings presents for good children, but who punishes the naughty children?'

'`Punishes?`' Cole gave her an odd look, but she remained transfixed by the poem. 'Well, there's always Black Peter, but I've never heard of a Without Man. He sounds more suited to Halloween.'

'It *belongs*.' Polly stressed huffily, and closed the book with a snap.

———

December 20th: Five days 'til Christmas

'You shouldn't bite your fingernails. It's a nasty habit.'

Cole looked up from the television, and followed his aunt's eye to the fingernails he had unconsciously been chewing. He laid both hands flat on his lap, resisting the urge to curl them into fists to hide the evidence of his compulsion. 'I know. I'm seeing a doctor about it.'

'Is that helping?'

He shrugged noncommittally. 'Kind of. I have a little notepad I carry round with me that I'm meant to draw in when I'm bored or whatever. It gives me something to do with my hands. It works if I need to hold the pad and pen, but if I'm sitting or at a table I still bite my off-hand.'

He held out his hands for comparison. While neither were a particularly attractive sight, the nails being worn down to the ragged skin, the left hand was noticeably worse, with most of the fingertips looking red and raw.

'Well,' Aunt Judith smiled, 'If you're looking for something to do with your hands, you could go check the outside decorations. I think some of them fell down in the storm last night.'

Prior to the conversation, Cole hadn't been looking for anything to occupy his hands, and he didn't much relish the thought of trudging about in the snow to rescue some slightly tacky plastic decorations, but not wanting to be rude, he instead said, 'Sure. I'll ask Polly if she wants to help, she likes doing Christmas decorations.'

As it transpired, the proposal didn't appeal to Polly either, being much more inclined to make snow angels and throw snow balls at him. Eventually, a compromise was reached; she wouldn't keep pelting him, and in return he would leave her to read her book on the steps down to the front gate while he poked about in the snow.

He had just helped a cheery, red-cheeked Santa get upright again when the rhythmic crunching of snow foretold someone passing by. While he normally wouldn't have taken much notice, the footsteps came to a halt by the gate, and a stranger's voice greeted his sister.

Turning around, he could see a boy of around his own age leaning on the gate. The boy was pale, with a splash of freckles across his nose, and jaw-length blond hair that was swept to one side. He had a strong jaw-line, though otherwise his features were soft, and was dressed in grey jeans and a thick, plain white jumper that was several sizes too large for him. The bottom of it hugged his thighs while the sleeves had been rolled up several times to accommodate his arms.

'My name's Troy. What's yours?' The stranger was saying. 'Do you live here? I've never seen you before.'

'Polly...' Cole stamped his way over. 'This is my brother, Cole.'

Troy glanced at him, nodded, smiled. Cole didn't return it.

'What're you reading?'

'A book Cole made for me. He drew all the pictures.' She turned it 'round to show him, hesitant, but polite.

'They're very good.' Troy's eyes slid back up to Cole's. 'You're very good, how old are you?'

'Fourteen.' Soon to be fifteen, but he disliked Troy's inquisitive manner and didn't indulge him further.

'Only fourteen.' Troy mused, despite the fact there couldn't have been more than a year or two between them. Cole amended his mental appraisal of the other boy to be nosy and patronising. Returning his attention to Polly, Troy added, 'Is it a book of Christmas Carols? I love Christmas Carols.'

'Yeah, carols and poems.'

'Does it have 'Away in a Manger'? That's my favourite.' The question was innocent, off-hand, but for some reason it made him feel uncomfortable, as though Troy already knew the answer and was directing the conversation somewhere.

Polly scuffed the toe of her boot in the snow, a clear sign that she was feeling awkward. 'No. Sorry...'

'Really? I could write it down for you. Cole can add it to your book later.' Troy's eyes flicked towards the outline of the notepad in Cole's pocket, and once more he had the strange sense that the boy was already aware of the answer. 'Do you have some paper I could borrow? A pen?'

Cole acquiesced, more out of a desire to get the stranger moving as soon as possible as anything else, and handed over his small notepad and pen.

Troy held the pen awkwardly, as though unused to writing, though perhaps it was simply the cold biting at his bare fingers, for the writing itself looked quick and precise. He went to hand paper and pen to Polly over the gate, but Cole intercepted them.

In neat, slanted writing were the words:

> *Away in a manger,*
> *No crib for a bed,*
> *The little Lord without*
> *Fingers, stomach, and head;*
> *The stars in the bright sky*
> *Look down where he lay,*
> *The little Lord without*
> *Life by the new day.*

A cold feeling that had nothing to do with the snow seeping through his boots swept over him, and his teeth clenched. 'What's this?'

'A carol. A poem.' Troy smiled, but there was no warmth to it, and it seemed more the result of a pained muscular spasm. 'I like it.'

Cole ripped the paper out and crumpled it into a ball one-handed. 'And you can keep it. I think you should leave. Now.'

Polly tugged at his arm. 'Cole, what's wrong?'

Troy's smile faded, but he made no move to leave. Cole took a step forward, off the steps, so that all that stood between him and Troy was four inches and one waist-high iron gate. 'Stay away from me and my sister.'

Cole did not cut an especially intimidating figure, being neither tall nor bulky for his age, giving the other boy at least three inches on him. Troy met his gaze, then flinched, something flickering in his eyes as he shrank away. 'I'm just trying to be nice.'

'I think Polly'd rather be without your particular version of 'nice'.'

'I was just being friendly. I like that carol. I wanted to share it. Isn't that what friends do? Share things?'

'I'm serious.' Cole replied coolly. 'Leave my sister *alone*.'

'Or *what*?' Though Troy still stood with his shoulders hunched, shrinking in on himself, his eyes were hard, and a sneer curled his lip. 'You sound like you'd do something, Cole, something bad. You wouldn't want to do something naughty, would you, Cole? So close to Christmas?'

'Please just leave.' Troy's eyes continued to drill into him, silently, then as suddenly as it had appeared the peculiar intensity was gone, and Troy was just an average, awkward boy with his gaze locked on his boots.

'Okay. I'm sorry for whatever I did. Maybe I'll see you tomorrow.'

'We're busy tomorrow.' Cole lied, but Troy gave no indication of having heard, and had started off down the street, humming something under his breath in time to his crunching steps as he did.

December 21st: Four days 'til Christmas

Cole had taken to spending most of his time in the study, where he could sit at the desk with his drawing pad, staring out the window in front of him at the grey clouds heavy with snow that made it seem later than it was. Polly, as far as he knew, was down the hall in the lounge, watching some cartoon or another.

He balanced his head on the palm of his hand, fingers resting at his lip and nails tapping against his teeth, though he paid little attention to this until something caught his eye at the window, and he bit down too hard in his sudden consternation. A strip of flesh came away in his teeth, leaving a sharp sting and angry, bloodied skin in its wake. He swore, glaring at his finger then back at the window.

He leaned forward, close enough that his breath misted the glass, and this was what outlined the hand-print on the window.

At first Cole thought the hand simply had very small fingers, and wondered if Polly had drawn it. Then, his mind drew back to what he thought he'd glimpsed, and his heart skipped a beat.

He stood slowly, peering into the darkness that blanketed the garden. For a long moment, he thought he'd imagined it... and then he saw it.

A tall, thin figure stood down the end of the garden. It stood so still that at first Cole had missed it, but then the wind blew, and the figure in the garden was the only thing that did not move. It was cast in deep shadow, making its state of dress impossible to determine—though he had the sudden impression it didn't require clothes to preserve its sexless modesty. He couldn't say where the thought came from.

It caved in alarmingly at the stomach, and he could see the silhouette of spine connecting the torso and pelvis. Awkward, stunted hands rested at its sides, the fingers far too short—no, he thought. Not fingers, *stumps*, ten stumps cut off at the first knuckle.

No fingers. No fingers to touch, or to take.

The neck of the creature opened up into the beginning slope of the lower jaw, yet reached no further, as though the rest of the head had been sliced off at the base of the chin. Something flopped uselessly out the side. A tongue, Cole realised, and, as if it sensed his scrutiny, it twitched and flicked upwards.

The Without Man tasted the air, yet made no other movement.

Then, beside him, a soft voice wormed itself into his ear, 'Stop biting your nails, Cole, or *you* won't have any fingers left either.'

Cole whipped 'round, staring at the boy beside him. Though his every instinct screamed not to look away, he chanced a glance at the window... but the Without Man was gone. His words, when he blurted them out, were breathy and tight with fear, and that realisation made him angry. '*You*. What are you doing here? How did you—' He broke off. He remembered the carol, the boy's hard, malevolent eyes... the sense of something not quite right. 'Who are you? Who is the Without Man?'

'Who?' Troy pondered, 'Or what? Think of him as... a herald. I made him, you see.'

'Made?'

A spasm of some emotion flitted across Troy's face. He closed his eyes, and jerked his head violently to one side as though trying to shake some thought from his head. 'He was a bad boy. He was naughty a long time ago, and he was punished. I was always a good boy. It's the duty of the good to punish the wicked. To make them repent. Do you see?'

'No.' Cole was sharp in his vehemence. 'No, and I don't want to. Isn't the place of good to forgive?'

Troy smiled wistfully. 'That's a shame, Cole. It'd be so much easier if you understood. She needs to be punished, you see.'

'She.' He repeated. 'Polly? What the hell d'you mean, 'punished'?'

Troy only gave him a beatific smile, and started forwards. Cole made to grab for him, only to clutch empty air as Troy ducked with freakish speed under his arm. He spun, angry, swinging his arm back as he did to strike Troy from behind, but the words forming on his lips died in his mouth as he found himself faced with an empty room, with only the gooseflesh that crept up his arms to give any indication that it had not all been his imagination.

He remained frozen, tense, and awkward, until suddenly he heard footsteps in the hall. The light that had previously crept out under the hallway door snuffed out with a tinkle of glass, succeeded by a sudden thud.

Polly screamed.

He ran to the door, yanking it open and almost crashing into an ashen-faced Polly. Droplets of blood ran down her cheek from a shallow cut on her cheekbone.

Cole grasped her by the arms. 'Are you okay? What happened?'

'Nothing.' She answered, but her answer came too quickly to be entirely truthful. She raised a hand to her cheek, brushing it against the cut. 'The light blew. The bulb exploded, and I got hit by the glass. It frightened me, that's all.'

He didn't believe her, but there was nothing he could say without telling her what he'd seen, and he had no intention of scaring her further.

He let the matter drop.

———

December 22nd: Three days 'til Christmas

On their first day down, Polly had made a chain of paper angels, which their Aunt had promptly—and proudly—hung. These angels were the first things that caught his eye as they entered the dining room.

They still clasped one another with tiny, paper hands, yet each one's head had been torn off, and their stomachs were marked with a gaping tear. They were only lifeless paper, and Cole could have sworn there was no breeze, yet they seemed to sway softly, dancing to some unheard music.

Perhaps a carol, Cole thought, perhaps the Without Man's tune, and the thought disturbed him.

Polly did not appear to have noticed, and so he did not point it out. Indeed, she seemed barely aware of what he was doing at all, her own eyes jumping from corner to corner, hand twitching and fidgeting with the scarf about her neck and her nails twisting and pulling at the fabric. Though there was no obvious source, he shared her apprehension.

It felt as though there were something just outside his field of vision, but whenever he turned to look, there was nothing there. This came accompanied by a growing feeling of pressure on his eyeballs, and he felt, bizarrely, as though someone were pressing on them, forcing certain images out.

Polly shivered beside him, and he noticed her fingers fluttering at her cheek, brushing against the plasters as if seeking either comfort or confirmation from them.

'Hi, Cole.' said a voice behind them. 'Polly.'

Cole turned slowly. He heard Polly stepping sideways, towards the door.

Troy stood in front of them, his attention focused on the knife in his right hand. He held it by the blade, and turned it this way and that, examining it carefully in the light. 'This is a lovely knife, isn't it? And old. Very old. I wonder where your Aunt got it from? It's handmade you know, well, the handle at least. I think it's made from holly wood. Probably because it's an easy wood to carve. Appropriate for the season as well, though I suppose that might just be coincidence.'

'The door won't open.' Polly whispered behind him.

There was no reason it shouldn't. It didn't even have a lock.

Cole's attention was fully focused on the knife. His heart raced, but time itself seemed to have slowed, the brief silence stretching out agonisingly before them. Troy seemed almost to have forgotten Cole's presence, and stood frozen, still holding the knife, his head turned towards Polly. He made no movements, and did not blink—nor seem to breathe.

'You were a naughty girl, Polly.' Troy spoke, and it sounded like an intonation. 'Naughty children have to be punished, that's the way of the world.'

His arm jerked at his side, sleeve unfolding and swallowing his hand as it did. He didn't seem to notice. He raised his hand, slowly taking hold of the blade's handle, trapping the soft wool of the jumper between wood and flesh.

'What the hell are you talking about?' Cole stepped in front of Polly protectively, one hand tentatively raised in a pacifying gesture. Troy ignored him, looked *through* him, eyes still focused on Polly's.

'You were naughty.' Troy repeated. 'It's naughty to open your presents early.'

Cole stared at him. 'Is this about the book? Look, I gave her the book, and I told her she could open it.'

Troy's head jerked upwards, his eyes finally settling on Cole's. 'Really?'

'Yes. So it's fine.' He felt Polly grip his arm and squeak his name, but her unspoken warning was too late.

'You voiced permission to take temptation. So the blame—the wrongdoing—is equally yours.' Troy nodded to himself, reversing the knife in his hands and tapping the tip of the blade against his lip. 'Do you know why the Without Man is without fingers? It's because he was naughty. He opened his presents before Christmas, and so his fingers had to be removed. The punishment fitting the crime, Cole.'

Cole could hear Polly hammering on the door, shouting, but Troy seemed untroubled by her efforts. Even if their Aunt could hear them, he was sure she could not get past the door. Being in the centre of the house, there were no windows, only the doors at opposing ends.

He felt light-headed, his hands cold and clammy. The temperature in the room was low, too low, and his breath puffed out before him when he spoke. 'And his stomach? His head?'

'Eating what wasn't for him. Christmas treats. A gluttonous stomach, greedy fingers. They're all signs of larger sins, Cole. As for his head? Pride. Assuming he could do what he liked. It's been a long time though. Sometimes it's… hard to remember.' Troy's hands tightened on the knife. 'But he *was* naughty.'

He could hear banging being reciprocated now, but it was too far away, separated by at least another door. He thought he could hear muffled shouting, but he couldn't catch the words, only their names, repeated with growing urgency.

Without warning, Troy lunged at him. Cole swung his arms up to fend him off, and this was his undoing, for Troy hadn't been springing to attack. Instead, he grabbed his outstretched arm, pulling him with surprising strength towards the dining table. Polly grabbed his other arm, and tried to pull him away, to no avail.

Troy forced his hand down on the table.

Cole struggled, desperately trying to gain the leverage to pull himself free, but Troy had the strength of something far older than the form he wore, and could have been carved from stone for all Cole managed to shift him.

Troy raised the knife left-handed, his intent suddenly crystallising in Cole's mind with horrible clarity.

'No!' Cole screamed, 'Please!'

Troy's fingers pressed his own against the wood. All Cole saw of the knife was a blur, and the glint of light on metal, then there was a dull thud as the blade cut through flesh and bone into the solid wood of the table beneath it, and Polly's scream echoed his own.

'Leave him alone!' she shrieked, 'LEAVE HIM ALONE!'

She launched herself at Troy, grabbing his arm and biting down hard. The flesh gave way beneath her teeth, the skin giving little resistance before breaking, but Troy showed no sign of discomfort or pain. He released the knife, sparing Polly a cursory glance before grabbing her by her dark curls to wrench her off his arm.

Cole shook violently, half-collapsed over the table and breathing in quick, pained, hiccupping gasps. His hand felt hot, too hot, searing warmth lancing up his arm and threatening to overwhelm him. Blood oozed forth, pooling about his hand and already beginning to sink into the grain of the table. Through blurred eyes he could make out his middle finger, the edges of the skin ragged and dead despite the cut being clean only moments before.

Above the pounding in his ears he heard Polly scream again in the background, and the sound spurred him on. He grabbed the knife with his uninjured hand, but it was embedded in the table with such force that he was unable to dislodge it. With one particularly violent wrench it snapped in his hand, leaving Cole with only the useless wooden handle. He registered this, dimly, and rather than thrusting forward made a clumsy, wild swing with the haft of it at Troy's temple.

He hit, but the angle was off and the handle scraped against the skin that struck it, yet Troy recoiled with a scream. He staggered to the side, one hand clutching at his head, pulled further off-balance by Polly. Whether by inspiration or chance her leg caught his, and Troy fell, pulling Polly with him.

Fear and adrenaline surged through Cole's system, fighting back the nausea and dizziness, and he half lunged, half fell on the boy—thing—before him, straddling his chest and raining blows down on his—its—face with the end of the handle. His vision blurred and spotted, but though he could not see it, he heard the crunch of bone as the nose was smashed by the handle, the wet, sucking sound as the wood sunk into the eye-socket, coming away damp and dark with blood and vitreous. White flesh flecked and blurred with red, and he could hear Polly hammering on the door, screaming.

The thing beneath him continued to keen in pain, and when his eyes cleared briefly as tears tracked down his cheek he thought he could see the flesh sizzling and bubbling where the wood had touched it. Then, finally, the thing grew silent, though Cole continued to beat it until the dull, throbbing pain of his shoulder almost rivalled the sharp, burning pain of his hand.

The thing was still, though whether dead or unconscious, he could not tell. He pushed himself upright on unsteady legs, vaguely aware of Polly saying something, of her trying to guide him away but he could not make out the words.

'The door,' She said, and the words seemed to come as though from far away. 'It opened. Quick, come on, *please.*'

The black threatened to swallow his vision, but somehow he managed to stagger out of the room. He noted his aunt rushing towards them, felt her arms enfold him as he collapsed.

As he fell, he turned his head back to the room, and the last thing he noticed before he passed out was the absence of a form on the floor.

––––––––

Unfriendly eyes watched them leave from the shadows, cradling the fallen form, taking its hands and gently entwining spectral fingers with the stumps. The other hand ghosted over where the cheek would be, had the form a head. Soothingly, lovingly, it spoke to the Without Man.

'Ssh, my darling. My poor dear. You were a good boy this year, my darling, I won't punish you. Someone else will punish the naughty children, someone always does. That's the way of the world. Do you hear that, Troy, my darling? Mother still loves you.'

––––––––

December 23rd: Two days 'til Christmas

They'd told his parents and the hospital staff that the amputation had been accidental, and his own fault. It seemed easier.

'You can go home tomorrow evening,' The nurse told him, 'In time for Christmas.'

Cole spent the rest of the evening curled in on himself, crying.

––––––––

December 24th: Christmas Eve

Polly sat at the end of his bed, reading aloud from the book balanced on her knee. In years past, the book was always a Christmas story, and they would take turns reading the chapters. This year, the book was 'The Wind in the Willows', and she had yet to offer it to him.

She avoided his eye, and when he reached out to her with his maimed hand she shied away from him, the words of the story slipping awkward and stilted from her mouth. He closed his eyes and pretended not to see the desperate, eager cast to her face as their mother's footsteps sounded down the hall, nor did he speak when there was a soft knock at the door, accompanied by a softer voice entreating his sister to go to bed. He closed his ears to the creaking of the chair as she stood, and to the whisper of her slippers across the floor as she began to move away, only to lose even this as the ringing of church bells crept into the edge of hearing, announcing the hour before midnight; the hour before Christmas day.

The distant clanging of bells turned to melodic chiming, the sound dancing and ringing about the room, merry and bright. As the last resounding notes echoed themselves into silence, a small, warm hand found his on the cover, tentative fingers mindful of his bandages, and held his hand 'til the tears he hadn't realised he'd been crying had dried on his cheeks, and dreamless sleep brought with it some semblance of comfort and peace.

CHRISTMAS GLITCH
by Carl Lambein Jr

It was December the Twenty-fifth and a light snow fell steadily across the coldest parts of the world just in time for the holidays. Inside his spacious home at The North Pole, S. Claus peeled off the layers of his thermal clothing, stepped into his spa-sized shower, letting the water cascade over his exhausted body, and washed off the grime of the world. Drying off, he eyed his chiseled six-foot-four-inch frame in the bathroom's full-length mirror. Pretty good for a twenty year old, let alone an eight-hundred-year-old legend!

Claus shaved, liberally splashing on his favorite aftershave—a present from his adoring wife. He smiled at his reflection: wavy blonde hair, high polished forehead, and deep-set blue eyes with a twinkle he had mastered over the decades. Perfection!

Wrapped in his red velour robe, he headed into his cozy, well-appointed office and poured himself a stiff Scotch—a reward for a job well done. After all, it was by no means an easy feat delivering toys to every kid in the world in one night. He had definitely earned the millions deposited in his off-shore accounts—millions paid by grateful toy companies for his continued years of loyal service.

Settling into his favorite recliner, he gazed contentedly into the fire crackling in the fireplace and was about to savor his first warm sip of scotch when a desperate knock came at his door. 'Enter!' he barked.

Everett Green—Head Elf, and Claus' right arm—scurried into the room, a grim look on his diminutive face.

'Pooch,' smiled Claus, 'why the sad face?'

The elf, never comfortable with his boss's habit of nicknaming the staff after canines, inwardly cringed. 'Ch-chief' he stammered, his agitated elfin voice soaring to a squeaky timber, 'we got ourselves a problem!'

Claus set down his drink, the twinkle in his eye gone. 'What do you mean 'we've got a problem'? I'm not back here an hour from my most demanding night of the year when you...'

Claus took a deep breath, observing the elf's trembling knees.

Yes, Everett was afraid—afraid to the point of passing out. He knew all too well what happened to those who failed to carry out The Boss' orders. In fact, his predecessor had 'disappeared' after a run-in with a hellion reindeer named Rudolph. There was no question Mr. S. Claus did not take 'problems' in a kind vein.

Summoning his courage, Everett declared, 'Ch-chief, there's a kid in Yeehaw Junction, Georgia, U.S. of A. who got overlooked. Our GPS has highlighted the location.'

Claus' eyes narrowed. Begrudgingly, he rose from his recliner, taking his scotch, and strode to his desk. Dropping down in his swivel chair, he set down his glass and pressed a button, bringing up a gigantic world map on a wall-mounted flat screen. Zeroing in on the United States, a red light appeared, pinpointing the Gilliam residence, 3224 Ogdon Street, Yeehaw Junction, Georgia.

Slowly Claus turned to the elf. 'How can this be?' His voice grew to an ear-splitting volume. 'Are you saying that *I*, The Great Claus, missed a house? Do you dare infer that I...'

'Oh, no, sir!' squeaked Everett. 'Never your mistake, sir! Has to be a glitch in the GPS system on the sleigh. It's being serviced as we speak!'

'Who's checking it out?'

'Nicky Kringle, sir. As you know, he's head of Tracking And Surveillance.'

Claus' mighty chest swelled. 'I knew it! *Dingo*! I should have known he was involved if there was a screw up. That elfin twerp must have sabotaged my sleigh!'

'Oh, no!' squeaked Everett. 'I mean, no, *sir*! I don't believe Dingo—I mean, Nicky—is capable of such an act. He has been nothing but loyal, sir. He... ' Suddenly, the elf clamped his mouth shut, weighing the cost of arguing with the boss. Inwardly he shuddered at the thought of poor Nicky's fate.

Nicholas 'Dingo' Kringle was a freak of elfin nature. Standing at five feet four inches tall, he towered over the other elves and was, in Claus' words, 'a miserable, meddling, mischievous troublemaker.' But he was also brilliant, with a mind like a calculator and an interest in computers as soon as he could crawl. When it came to CPUs or software engineering, there was no question Nicholas Kringle was the elf for the job. Unfortunately, his honesty and unbridled enthusiasm invariably put him on The Boss' bad side. More than once he got up in Claus' sleigh runners about this or that: *The elves aren't getting enough pay—maybe they should unionize; The reindeer's diet should include more fiber; Mrs. C. sure looks hot in that purple snowsuit!* No matter what came out of Nicky's mouth, it was bound to perturb The Boss.

Claus pulled up 'Files' on his computer. Clicking on 'Pups'—his codename for elves — he entered 'Nicholas K. Kringle'. Up popped three pages which made Claus shake his mighty head. 'Pooch, explain this last entry concerning Dingo and Rudolph.'

Everett sucked in a deep breath through clenched teeth. He had hoped this particular infraction would have gone unnoticed. 'Well, sir,' he began, 'Nicky released Rudolph from his stall to take the creature for a walk. But the beast headed straight for the other reindeer and before he could be corralled, he killed two bucks. Sir, might I remind you, Rudolph is an alpha male, only following his instincts, and...'

'You don't need remind me of anything, Pooch!' snapped Claus. 'I've followed that brute from the moment he was foaled. He's been a menace to my herd from the start, especially during rutting season. As I recall, he nearly crushed two of my prize females. If he weren't such an outstanding stud, I'd have turned his hide into a coat years ago! And as for Dingo. That freakin' elf... '

'Sir,' interrupted Everett, attempting a diversion, 'I don't like telling tales out of school, but Rudolph has, uh…failed to inseminate his last two does. Old age? Maybe, sir, but I do know the beast's appetite hasn't faltered. He eats at least three times as much as any other reindeer, costing you a fortune. And his special housing is expensive, too. And that shiny red nose of his is such a distraction. In all honesty, Boss, I have to question whether Rudolph is pulling his weight.'

Claus glared at the elf. 'Are you suggesting we put Rudolph down?'

'Oh, no sir,' squeaked Everett, backpedalling. 'Just stating facts, sir. I make no suggestions. Oh, no, never!'

Claus downed his scotch in a single gulp. 'Go and collect that birdbrain, Dingo. Bring him here immediately, if not sooner!'

'Yes, sir!' squeaked Everett, and rocketed from the office.

Claus stared pensively at the map on his flat screen, his blood pressure rising. Suddenly, inside the chimney there arose such a clatter he sprang from his chair to see what was the matter. As he jerked his head and swiveled around, down the chimney Nicholas Kringle came with a bound!

'What the *bleep!* gasped Claus. 'How the hell did you do *that?*'

Nicky, his full white beard sparkling with new fallen snow, brushed a bit of soot off his green uniform. 'It's a neat trick, isn't it, sir? I can teach it to you if you like.' I got the idea from a poem I read once. Let's see, I think it went something like, "Twas the night before Christmas, when all through the house, not a creature was stirring, not even a…"'

'Never mind that, you nitwit!' barked Claus. He dropped back down in his chair. 'Get your fat as over here, NOW!'

'Yes, sir!' said Nicky. He hurried to Claus' desk and snapped to attention. 'You wanted to see me, sir?'

Leaning back, Claus folded his massive arms and said in a surprisingly calm voice, 'Why, yes, Dingo, I did want to see you. What have you found out concerning our little 'error' in Georgia?'

'Well, we're still working on it, sir. Can't seem to find the problem. There's no glitch in the system. I just don't get it.'

'You were the one who programmed the trip?'

'Yes, sir, I did. But I've run a complete diagnostics, and found no errors. That leaves only one possibility, sir. With all due respect, I believe you… missed the stop.'

A look of extreme contempt crossed Claus' face, but then, strangely, his fierce expression dissolved into one of utter contentment. 'You know,' he said matter-of-factly, 'I've never made a mistake before. But perhaps I'm not so perfect after all. Could be I just forgot. Well, Dingo, old man, we can't let that poor little child in Georgia down now, can we. You go saddle up Rudolph—you seem to be so fond of the beast—and deliver the toys to Yeehaw Junction yourself.'

For a moment Nicky stood motionless, unsure of how to process the directive, but then, seeing no alternative, he saluted and headed for the reindeer stalls. There was no question in his mind his tracking system hadn't failed, but he was on thin ice with The Boss as it was, and he knew arguing with him would have been fruitless, if not downright dangerous.

Inside the North Pole's main barn Nicky donned his cold weather gear: thermal layers of clothing underneath a red velvet suit trimmed in white fur with a matching hat. Then, he fitted the traditional green leather harness around Rudolph, feeding him a reindeer treat for good measure. And finally, at the runway, after being sprayed down with turbo juice, the duo and their enchanted sleigh were rendered invisible by a cloaking device and sent off into the night sky.

Claus poured himself another scotch and settled back in his desk chair to track the sleigh on his world map. The magic transport was at warp speed, already well past Iceland and approaching the U.S. over the Atlantic. As it neared the Washington, DC area, Claus swung over to his control panel and pushed a button, removing the sleigh's cloaking device. He typed in 'Russian MIG' and hit 'Enter'. It took NORAD less than two minutes to scramble what, from the blips on Claus' screen, numbered three Marine F-4 Phantom Jets sent to intercept the 'bogie' flying in restricted air space. In seconds the jets closed in on what they identified as a UFO, and instantly only three blips remained, the fourth having disappeared entirely.

Claus shut down his screen. With a broad smile of satisfaction, he was about to reach for his scotch when he noticed his wife seated in his recliner. 'Sweetheart, how long have you been there?'

'Long enough to see you manipulate your control panel again. Just whom did you remove this time?'

Claus locked eyes with his wife. 'Now lovey, you know sometimes I have to do some rather unpleasant things to maintain status quo around here. I had no choice but to eliminate Dingo and Rudolph. They had outlived their usefulness.'

A slow smile crossed Mrs. Claus' face. 'I believe *you* are the one who's outlived his usefulness, my dear.'

Suddenly, the massive door to Claus' office opened and in walked Nicholas Kringle, very much intact. 'I always was a mischievous elf, sir. You said so yourself. Too bad you put me in charge of your computer program. Too bad for *you*, that is.'

Claus' face turned red as the holly berries decorating his fireplace mantle. Fury ignited his instincts and he shot out from behind his desk, his expression contorting into a devilish sneer. With a powerful roar, he threw himself at the elf, the impact sending them both to the ground.

But Nicky had not come alone.

In the doorway there appeared a gigantic reindeer, his nostrils flared, his antlers poised...for a lethal charge!

THE EGG MAN
by Fiona Moore

Boxing Day, 1974. Joe unhitched his seat belt and pulled himself out of the wreckage of the intercity coach. The wind seared through his brown polyester uniform (too thin of course, even for wearing on the coach, but One Must Make Sacrifices as his boss said) and the snow drove into his face.

His head hurt and he touched it. No blood, must just be a bruise. Felt pretty sore to be a bruise, but never mind. His legs and arms seemed to work OK, if a little weak and wobbly.

He sat, dazed, on the left front wheel for a few minutes and surveyed the damage. Was anybody hurt? he wondered finally. Had anybody else been on the coach? He thought he remembered a fat old lady and a teenage boy, sitting at the back. Carefully, he stood up, steeled himself, clambered back in. 'Hello?' he called stupidly. 'Anyone there'?

The coach was empty. So either there hadn't actually been any passengers, or else the old lady and the boy had got themselves out and away while he'd been unconscious. Good. Joe had been given first aid training, which was to say that a manager had told him where the box of bandages was located, and so he was very grateful not to have to put it to use, especially not on a day like this.

He climbed shakily out again, took stock. The blowing snow was getting worse, but from the looks of things they'd gone over the edge on the tricky bit of road that bordered the old quarry. No point in staying here; he'd be frozen before anybody missed him at the best of times, and on a holiday... well. Plus with this snowstorm (blowing up out of the month's mild weather like something conjured), the emergency services would all be busy elsewhere. His best hope was to strike out for the edge of the quarry, he was pretty sure there was an emergency call-box at the lay-by at the bottom of the road.

Joe turned up his collar and started pushing, one foot in front of the other, into the freezing white unknown.

A few minutes later he realised he'd left his hat behind, but he was no longer sure where the coach was, so he didn't bother going back for it.

It had been seven years ago that the trouble had started. Seven years ago that day, in fact. Boxing Day, 1967. His parents had been speaking to him again, so he and Moonflower had decided to spend Christmas with them instead of down at the squat. They'd mostly spent two days giggling about how hopelessly, almost comedically square the whole thing was, guest bedrooms and sheer curtains and people complaining about how the butcher got the order wrong, or the milkman was late, or some other tradesman was somehow letting them down.

Boxing Day, they'd smoked a not-terribly-surreptitious joint behind the garden shed before going in to watch the main event—the Beatles' new telemovie, *The Magical Mystery Tour*. His parents had gone round the neighbours', muttering about Joe's rudeness in not joining them, so he and Moonflower lounged, pleasantly stoned, on the overstuffed sofa watching the images on the flickering black-and-white television.

He couldn't say this of course, but, for a moment, the film had opened up a new reality. Like a window that opened up in the television, then opened more windows in his head. It had started when Ringo, holding his ticket for the tour, turned around and looked out through the screen and smiled, and Joe knew, really knew, that Ringo was looking at *him*.

The film unfolded, the story of the fat lady and the old man, and the little girl, and the accordion player, and the starlet, and the band: Paul as a Fool, John as a dark magician, Ringo as a loveable bloke and George as, well, George, the hippopotamus and the bird and the rabbit and the walrus. All on the bus, travelling through magical moon-landscapes and dream worlds, with the courier in his white hat and white uniforms, cracking jokes and leading songs, while around him, the narration enthused, everybody was having a lovely time.

And behind it all, orchestrating everything, the four wizards, earth and sky and fire and water, weaving their magic to create a new universe, where nothing made sense but it was okay. And Joe knew, really knew in a way he'd never known anything before, that those wizards really were there, building that world, taking that tour, making everything all right so everyone, not just the people on the bus but everyone who believed, could have a lovely time.

And although he knew he couldn't have, although everyone else would tell him this could never be the case, Joe was positive he'd seen it in colour.

As the last chord faded and the newsreaders took over the screen, the pair of them sat dreamily for a minute, caught in the enchantment, not daring, or not able, to break the spell.

And then Moonflower stretched and turned to Joe. 'Well,' she said. 'That was nice.'

She sounded like she had just been watching a school play, or been for tea at the neighbours'. Joe nodded, unable to say anything, especially not about the feeling which had just opened up in his stomach, the black instinctive knowledge that *something was wrong*.

The something that was wrong expanded almost immediately after they got home from his parents' and found that the owner of the squat had quietly moved back in and retaken possession.

'We'll need to rent a flat,' Moonflower said among their bags, piled in front of the house on the dry and scrubby lawn.

'That'll cost money,' Joe pointed out. 'Which we don't have.'

'We can get jobs,' Moonflower said matter-of-factly, she who a few months earlier was scorning the entire capitalist system as bourgeois. 'I've still got a certificate from secretarial college.'

'What about me?'

Moonflower frowned a bit. 'I suppose you could become a postman or something.'

Moonflower got a job almost straight away, doing secretarial work for the local department store, and, after a couple of weeks of crashing on a friend's living-room floor, found them a flat. Joe drifted around a bit more but, under the pressure to do so, eventually found a job with the bus service. It was boring work but not unpleasant, and when he got really down about it, he could always pretend he was on the Magical Mystery Tour for a bit, though the reality always bled back in after a minute or two. He also had to admit it wasn't a bad thing having a flat, with reasonably reliable heating and water and without the constant threat of being kicked out over his head.

The problem was that Moonflower was now insisting he call her Julie.

At first only to her friends from work (boring people in brown polyester, drinking sepia cocktails), but then, eventually, she started to insist all the time. And then she began to talk about kids, and then getting married.

'What happened to marriage as a bourgeois patriarchal concept?' Joe asked.

'I'm just thinking, when we enrol the kids in school, it'll be much easier if we're married.'

'Who said we're going to have kids?' Joe asked, but he could see the way this was going even before, some weeks later, she announced she was leaving him for a junior sales manager with his very own bald spot. Joe got the flat, which he kept hopefully festooned with the drapes and lamps she'd bought for them back before the Mystery Tour.

But all around him things were going wrong. Suddenly, just as the televisions became colour, the colours all faded into browns and sepias, and the dreams of having a Quaker in the White House, and no more dependency on coal and oil, and nobody having any money, all came true, but not the way Joe had expected.

Joe himself wasn't doing too badly—there were layoffs at the bus company, and as an unenthusiastic worker who never turned up to union meetings Joe was one, but he had a clean record and five years' experience, which was enough to get a job with an intercity coach service. It was regular work but not continuous, and he could work the evening shift if he wanted, and he got extra money for working on holidays. But still, every time he boarded the drab green coach and settled into the brown-and-orange upholstery, every time he put on the polyester uniform or said

'Thank you' to another overtime bonus, he had the feeling that the strange bubble universe in which the Magical Mystery Tour had formed was moving further and further out of his grasp.

Sometimes, he would think he saw it. A coloured sign disappearing round a corner. A strange person—a fat lady, or an old man in a uniform, or a lanky blond man in a scarf—who would resolve into someone rather more ordinary. A wild drift of harmonizing voices on the air, turning into a burst from a passing in-car eight-track. He'd sometimes try to talk about it with the friends he was still in touch with, but they were increasingly uninterested in discussing surrealism and film and utopias, and kept turning the conversation to the cost of milk or the European Economic Community or the availability of Good Schools. Joe just kept on looking for the tour bus.

That time two Christmasses ago when he'd unwisely had a few double whiskies and started a fight in a pub with some kids who didn't like his hippie moustache, as he lay curled up bleeding in the gutter, that was when he came closest to it: he heard the music, saw the shape of the bus rolling up in a blaze of coloured lights and wild guitar. He felt strangely warm, and light; like he was in an egg, waiting to be born into a psychedelic reality, moving away, don't be long, don't be long don't belong don't belong don't belong—

Then a Northern voice said 'well, this one's right out of it, come on, give us a hand,' and he realised as he was lifted gently on a soft cloud that smelled of mothballs and wool that it was only the ambulance crew.

Through the blowing snow he could see it. Like a crack that opened up in the clouds, like the sky was breaking and heaven showing through. And he could see it.

See the four wizards.

The four benign wizards who had magicked up the Magical Mystery Tour. Peering through the breaking sky, looking down at him. Smiling.

Joe realized he'd been right.

The time he'd looked into the television and realised it was a whole other universe in the Magical Mystery Tour. It was right. There really was a magical mystery tour. It hadn't faded, it hadn't vanished. Somewhere, between the dimensions, the tour was going on. He was an egg man, he was the egg man, he was—

Joe collapsed to his knees in the snow. The wizards faded, but he could see it, in the sky. The bus, and all the people inside it. He wanted—it was hard to think now, but he wanted—he wanted to be there. If he could just have one wish, it would be for all this, the intercity coaches and flats and economic crises and quarries and earth-tone boredom to just *end*, to hatch out of this world and to spend forever out there, on the tour....

And he thought he saw it. Ringo, turning to face him, ticket in hand, smile on face. Only this time, he reached out to Joe, held out the ticket from the sky.

What did Joe have to lose? No girlfriend, no beautiful people anymore, friends all having jobs and marriages and children, his own tiny hold on capitalism (the flat, the job) growing like a brown melanoma on his skin, everything sepia, everything polyester, Paul writing pop-songs and the rest of them writing incomprehensible garbage. Don't even get him started about Yoko Ono. Nothing there anymore for him.

Joe took the ticket.

Reality broke open.

———————

And there he was on the bus. They were all there—the fat lady, and the little girl, and the accordion player and the old man, and the starlet, and the band, and the stripper, and Paul in his hat as the Fool, and they were all happy to see him.

There were other people too. His parents. Moonflower, back before she'd turned into Julie. His friends from the squat. Lots of other people he didn't know, but he had the feeling they'd get on just fine.

Joe then realized where he was.

He was standing up at the front by the driver. He was clad in white, a white hat and a white uniform, cracking jokes and leading songs, and everyone was laughing, and clapping, and the more jokes he told, the happier everyone was, and the happier he was too.

And everybody, simply *everybody,* was having a lovely time.

KILLER REINDEER
by Spencer Carvalho

Little Timmy and Sarah tried on previous Christmas Eve's to stay up all night so they could see Santa Claus but didn't make it. This year they stayed up past their bedtime with the help of Dutch energy drinks they bought online. They hid behind the couch across from their fireplace and waited for Santa's arrival.

Eventually they heard a loud thud from their roof and a clatter. They got up to see what was the matter. Then they heard something falling down the chimney. An overweight man in red and white somehow fell out of the chimney that was much too small for him. He landed face down and didn't move.

Little Timmy and Sarah slowly walked over to him. When they got closer to him they could see he was covered in bruises and blood. He groaned as he got to his hands and knees.

'Santa?' asked Timmy.

Santa looked up at Timmy. Santa looked worn down but still managed a smile.

'Merry Christmas,' said Santa.

Santa got up and staggered into the kitchen.

'We left out cookies and milk,' said Sarah. 'The cookies are gluten free.'

Santa Claus went past the cookies to the drawers and pulled out two very large stainless steel knives. He then looked at the children.

'Well, that's very nice of you to offer milk and cookies but I have something important to deal with first,' said Santa.

'What's that?' asked Timmy.

Santa walked back into the living room.

'The reindeer have rabies,' said Santa.

'What?' asked Timmy.

'They got attacked by some bats a while back,' said Santa. 'I guess some of the bats had rabies. Rabies isn't really a problem at the North Pole. I kind of figured the reindeer were immune to diseases since they're magic. Apparently not.'

Santa walked into the center of the living room ready for combat. He kept his back to the chimney.

'Are they going to come down the chimney?' asked Timmy.

'No, no, no,' said Santa. 'Reindeer can't fit down chimneys.'

'How did you fit down the chimney?' asked Sarah.

'Magic,' said Santa.

'Aren't the flying reindeer magic?' asked Timmy.

'It's a different kind of magic,' said Santa. 'You kids should wake up your parents.'

'They won't wake up,' said Timmy. 'They take drugs to sleep. They took sleeping pills. Nothing will wake them up.'

At that moment Dancer burst through the living room window knocking over the Christmas tree. He was foaming at the mouth and had a crazy look in his eyes. Dancer started growling.

'It's time to dance, Dancer,' said Santa.

Dancer charged him and got two stainless steel kitchen knives in the head for his trouble. The knives instantly killed him.

Prancer came in through the window next. Prancer ignored Santa and went for the children but Santa jumped in the way and grabbed the rabid reindeer by the horns. Santa locked eyes with Prancer and saw that there was nothing left but mania.

'You can't prance away from this,' said Santa.

Then Santa strained with all his might as he twisted the horns and snapped Prancer's neck. He stood over the dead reindeer.

'You kids probably weren't expecting this for Christmas,' said Santa. 'I'll make it up to you with…'

The wall around the living room window exploded as Comet shot through the window at full speed and hit Santa. They both flew through the living room and out the back wall into the back yard. Little Timmy and Sarah ran to the back yard to see Santa pinned to the ground with a rabid Comet over top of him. Santa was using both hands to hold Comet back from eating his face.

'Tis the season to help others,' said Santa.

Little Timmy and Sarah looked around for a way to help Santa. Timmy saw an icicle hanging nearby. He broke it off and tossed it to Santa who wrapped his jolly fingers around it and stabbed Comet in the neck. Comet bled out and collapsed.

'Are you okay Santa?' asked Sarah.

'Yes,' said Santa. 'But I have to deal with the rest of the rabid reindeer and save Christmas.'

Santa looked up towards the roof. They could see part of his sleigh.

'If I could get to my magic sack then I could get some weapons. We should get inside.'

The three went inside. Santa looked over to the fireplace.

'Should we call the cops?' asked Timmy.

'The cops aren't going to be able to help us, little guy,' said Santa. 'Don't worry though, I'll keep you safe.'

Santa Claus backed up to get a running start and ran full speed at the chimney and jumped into it. He somehow magically fit into it and shot right up to the top. Little Timmy and Sarah looked around at the two dead reindeer inside their living room and the two large holes in their walls, one leading to the front yard and the other leading to the back. They could hear fighting coming from the roof.

'Ho, ho, ho!' yelled Santa.

They heard a shotgun being fired and then Donner's lifeless body landed in their front yard. Then they could hear a chainsaw and the sound of meat being cut.

Blitzen's lifeless bloodied body landed in their front yard followed a second later by Blitzen's head. They heard a rocket fire and then saw the snowman in their yard blow up as the rocket missed its target. They heard a terrible racket of something tumbling off the roof and Santa landed in the yard.

'Santa!' yelled Sarah.

Cupid landed in the yard between Santa and the hole in the living room wall. He was bigger than the other reindeer. Cupid stared at Santa with his mouth foaming over. Santa could see the manic viciousness in his eyes.

'Cupid, you've always been my least favorite,' said Santa.

Dasher and Vixen landed in the yard next. They were also foaming at the mouth. All three started moving towards Santa.

'I could really use a Christmas miracle about now,' said Santa.

A Christmas tree ornament shattered across Cupid's head. Little Timmy and Sarah were throwing Christmas tree ornaments at the rabid reindeer. This distracted the reindeer but also made them very angry. They charged the kids. Santa tried to get to his feet to save the children but couldn't get up in time.

'No!' yelled Santa.

Dasher was the closest to little Timmy and Sarah. He was just feet away from little Timmy and Sarah when something landed on his head and crushed his skull. There was a blindingly bright red light that started to fade and when it finally died down the kids were able to see what it was. It was Rudolph, there to save the day.

'That's why you're my favorite, Rudolph,' said Santa.

Rudolph seemed to smile like he knew what Santa had said. Vixen moved in and Rudolph locked horns with her. They were face to face battling to the death. Rudolph was using all his strength to keep Vixen away from the children but Vixen was bigger than Rudolph and slowly pushed Rudolph back. His hooves slid across the ground. Rudolph was giving it everything he had but he was the smallest of the reindeer. Vixen was so much stronger.

'I love you Rudolph,' said Sarah.

Hearing that gave Rudolph the strength of ten reindeer and he knocked Vixen's head aside and jammed his horns into Vixen's heart. Vixen struggled but eventually stopped moving. Rudolph removed his horns from Vixen and looked at Cupid. Cupid was the largest and strongest of the reindeer. Rudolph was the smallest but had the biggest heart. Rudolph stood his ground.

There was nothing left of the old Cupid. Rabies had turned the magically flying reindeer into a killing machine. It was all madness and fury. It lowered its head to charge and Santa jumped on its back. Cupid started bucking but Santa grabbed Cupid's horns to hold on. Santa started repeatedly punching Cupid in the back of the head. Cupid threw Santa off his back and kicked him in mid air sending him against the side of the house. Rudolph attacked and cut Cupid's torso with his horns but Cupid kicked him aside.

'Rudolph!' yelled Sarah.

Rudolph didn't get up. Santa reached through the hole in the living room wall and picked up the Christmas tree. Cupid moved towards Rudolph and Santa swung the tree with all his might and smacked Cupid right in the face. Ornaments flew off the tree as he repeatedly hit Cupid with the Christmas tree. Cupid stabbed his horns into the Christmas tree and tossed it aside. He then kicked Santa and knocked him to the ground.

'I will not let you ruin Christmas!' yelled Timmy.

Little Timmy grabbed a candy cane that fell off his Christmas tree and broke the end off with his teeth making a festive shiv. He ran over and stabbed Cupid in the neck. Cupid started thrashing wildly and knocked little Timmy to the ground. Santa got up and grabbed the Christmas lights from the tree. Santa wrapped the Christmas tree lights around Cupid's neck. The two struggled but Santa did not let go.

'Go to sleep,' said Santa.

Santa choked Cupid to death.

'Is he dead?' asked Timmy finally.

'Yes Timmy, Cupid's dead,' said Santa.

Santa looked over at Rudolph who was lying injured. Sarah was petting him.

'How is he?' asked Santa.

'He'll be okay,' said Sarah.

Santa walked over to Rudolph. He kneeled down beside him and started petting him.

'Good boy,' said Santa. 'You're a very good boy.'

Rudolph got up and flew behind, as Santa staggered into the house and sat down at the kitchen table for some milk and cookies. Santa broke off a piece of a cookie and tossed it to Rudolph who ate it out of the air. Sarah continued petting Rudolph. Santa tried the cookies himself.

'These are actually pretty good,' said Santa. 'Gluten free?'

Santa drank some of the milk.

'Timmy wanted to leave a milkshake instead of milk,' said Sarah.

'What flavor?' asked Santa.

'Strawberry,' said Timmy.

'That would have been pretty good,' said Santa. 'Strawberry is my favorite flavor. There's always next year.'

Santa looked around at the destroyed house. There were holes in the walls, the Christmas tree was in the yard, and there were dead reindeer scattered about.

'This place is a mess,' said Santa. 'I'll send some elves to fix this place before your parents get up. They do great work and they're very fast.'

'Thanks Santa,' said little Timmy.

Santa looked Timmy in the eyes.

'Thank you Timmy,' said Santa. 'You two were very brave tonight. You both helped save Christmas.'

'Thanks Santa,' said Timmy.

'Yeah, thanks Santa,' said Sarah.

Sarah started trying to climb up onto Rudolph's back but was having trouble because she wasn't tall enough. Rudolph kneeled down and she climbed on. When she got on she hugged Rudolph's neck.

'If it is any consolation, you two are going to get great Christmas presents,' said Santa. 'Usually the nicer you are the better the gifts and it's pretty hard to top saving Christmas.'

'Will you still be able to deliver all the presents?' asked Sarah.

'Why, of course,' said Santa. 'I've still got one reindeer. That's enough. And after tonight I'll have a whole year to find new magic flying reindeer.'

Santa finished the milk and cookies.

'Now it's getting pretty late,' said Santa. 'I think it's time you kids got to bed.'

'You expect us to sleep after all this?' asked Timmy. 'We just helped Santa Claus fight off a group of rabid flying magic reindeer. This was the craziest night of my life. How can I sleep?'

Santa tilted his head toward Rudolph. Timmy looked over and saw that Sarah was asleep on Rudolph's back. Rudolph helped carry Sarah up to her bedroom. Timmy lifted her off Rudolph's back and made sure she was tucked in.

'I love you,' said Sarah.

'I love you too,' said Timmy.

'I was talking to Rudolph,' said Sarah.

Rudolph's nose shined a little brighter.

'I'm sure Rudolph loves you too,' said Timmy.

'Good,' said Sarah.

She rolled over and went to sleep. Timmy followed Rudolph to the living room so he could say goodbye but Santa was already gone. Rudolph flew out the living room and up to the roof. Timmy went to the edge of the living room where the hole was. He saw Santa's sleigh fly away into the night.

'Merry Christmas Santa!' yelled Timmy.

'Merry Christmas to all!' yelled Santa. 'And to all a good night!'

Timmy felt his Dutch energy drink wearing off so he went to bed. In the morning he and Sarah got up and went down to the living room. The holes were fixed and the dead reindeer were gone. There was a brand new Christmas tree that looked exactly like the old one. There was even a replacement snowman in the yard.

And the part that little Timmy and Sarah liked most?

It was the giant pile of presents.

PANTOCRIME

By Andrew Lawston

A shadow stood in the theatre wings under the cold white light of a fire exit, and tested the edge of a hefty axe. It was heavier than she'd expected, and looked absurd in her old hands, but it would certainly do the job.

In the still darkness, the theatre was a forbidding place. The faintest smears of light lent peculiar shades to otherwise cheery scenery, the weak illumination stumbling over the hasty brushwork to lend the flats the mottled texture of mouldy fruit. Out in the empty auditorium, rows of seats rustled with ghosts of audiences past. Or perhaps it was the rats.

When you're *hoping* a mysterious noise in the dark is a rat, you're in a dreary state, thought Rosie Hadfield, with a wry smile.

Rosie could just about hear the director's voice murmuring from the tinsel-strewn dressing rooms, the usual litany: treat the dress rehearsal as a real performance, go out and have fun, enjoy it, break a leg darlings. She could recite it, but the familiar sentiments would ground even the youngest actors, shift their attention away from the fact they were giving up the last Saturday before Christmas, and towards the performance they'd have to give very soon now.

Time to finish checking the props, in fact. Satisfied that Jack's rubber axe was in place, Rosie pushed her round glasses down over her silver curls to count the eggs in the carton for the bakery scene.

A rustling from the other side of the stage made Rosie glance up. Probably Flo, the prompt. She liked to settle down on her stool in plenty of time, penlight and script in hand, to get comfortable and to enjoy the sounds of the auditorium filling up as the audience took their seats. Even if the only audience tonight would be the producer and the front of house volunteers.

Rosie couldn't quite see Flo or the gleam of her torch, but the sound reminded her that she hadn't yet checked the smaller props table in the wings to stage left. Buttermilk's bucket had a tendency to go missing after the pantomime cow kicked it into the orchestra pit in Scene 3.

It wasn't her department, but as she crossed the stage, she stole a fascinated glance at the pyropots strung along the front to announce the various entrances of the wicked witch and the good fairy.

She started as she noticed a label. One of the pots was a firework rather than the smoke and glitter charge she'd expected! Fairy Sugarplum would give her opening speech from the dress circle if she was standing near that when it went off!

Not that the church hall they used as a theatre had a dress circle, of course, but that was hardly the point. Rosie's hands shook as she yanked the power cable from the pyropot. She dropped the firework and cable and stalked towards the dressing rooms. She'd averted a serious injury to a leading lady, but now she fully intended to inflict one on the technical crew.

She was intercepted outside the disabled toilet. Ingrid Lutwyche was possibly the most formidable director amateur dramatics had ever seen. Six foot tall, she towered over most of the actors, which was just how she liked it. She persisted in wearing tight black jeans and leather throughout the year, topped off with a dainty white scarf. The committee kept saying the group was lucky to have her, but they were a little shy of explaining exactly why. Her first production had been an all-female *Waiting for Godot*; she'd had to abandon *Charlie's Aunt* after she'd tried to persuade the cast to get naked for a trust-building exercise at the first rehearsal and they'd walked out *en masse*.

'Curtain in five, Rosie,' Ingrid said with a crisp nod that seemed more like a nervous twitch, sending her neat dark bob flicking about just out of sync with her head.

Rosie waved this away. 'Yes, I'm ready. Do you know who set up the pyropots? There's a socking great firework jammed in one of them!'

She wasn't sure what reaction she'd anticipated, but she hadn't expected Ingrid to start laughing. 'Oh, these silly first night pranks! Did you know both Bob F *and* Bob G in the cowsuit are wearing respirators because they each claim the other's farting?'

'Ingrid, I don't think you heard me, it was really dangerous.'

Ingrid was already walking away, and waved Rosie's warning aside with a shrug. 'Well, then we won't use the bangs and flashes tonight, they cost a fortune anyway.'

That was clearly that. A group where a dozen adults could spend three quarters of an hour deciding how to knock over a bottle would happily gloss over a potentially fatal incident.

Perhaps she was over-reacting, Rosie thought as she stomped back to the wings. The truth was, she was pretty bored. She'd turned up hours early to set up the props, and found most of them already in place following the technical rehearsal the day before. So she was hanging around with little to do, and couldn't even text her friends. Ingrid had demanded everyone hand over their phones so as not to be distracted.

Directors were supposed to be intense, but Ingrid had taken this show so *seriously,* which was odd given that pantomime was the last thing anyone thought she'd want to take on. As a rule, she wouldn't touch anything that might embarrass her if she bumped into Germaine or Bonnie Greer.

The show opened with a flurry of musical numbers, the frenzied activity on stage underlining how bored Rosie was getting in the wings. It was all rubbish kids' stuff, really, Ingrid had airbrushed all the more sophisticated jokes from the script. Rosie knew her history, and she couldn't help thinking it ought to be different. Pantomime had never been high art, but it had been full of bawdy humour, full of visual spectacle. Not for children, but somehow a lot more *fun*. The clown should be a chaotic, leaping, sausage-stealing giant like Grimaldi, not a chirpy idiot who couldn't dance.

There should be a bit of danger underneath all this banality, a sense that the fun was only one pratfall away from chaotic terror.

Full of these thoughts, Rosie looked out over the stage, where the wicked witch was picking up her broomstick for a dramatic exit. They'd spent ages looking at this little stunt, but decided that a full wire scene would be beyond their miniscule budget, and there wasn't enough space above the stage anyway. Wicked witch Megan Mog wasn't doing much more than an exaggerated hop into the wings, assisted by a sturdy stagehand yanking on the other end of a long rope.

'Fly away I will, and think of spells yucky
To cast on these fools - oi, don't be mucky!'

The last was in response to a hoped-for catcall as the witch flashed a stocking on mounting the broomstick. Rosie could feel Ingrid's stony glower even from backstage. She was surprised the dreadful woman hadn't cut even more of the racier gags.

Megan Mog, or Erin, gave her trademark cackle and jumped. But instead of lurching towards the wings, she soared straight up. As she was almost level with the top of the proscenium arch, the broomstick suddenly lurched back, spilling the terrified actress into the air.

Half a dozen alarmed shouts were cut off as Erin twisted desperately mid-fall and grabbed hold of a lighting bar by her fingertips.

The horrified silence was broken by Ingrid calling from the auditorium. 'Well done, Erin! Remember, if something like that does happen on the night, always keep it light, try to make a joke of it. The audience can never tell!'

Erin's face was contorted in pain, her knuckles white on the lighting bar. 'I can't feel me fingers,' she called.

'Yes, that's the stuff,' Ingrid replied, chuckling even as Erin's hands slipped and she plummeted towards the stage.

Before she even knew she was moving, Rosie had dashed on to the stage and driven her shoulder hard into the foam beanstalk. The giant ersatz weed crashed forward into Erin's path and broke her fall, leaving witch, broomstick and scenery in a jumbled heap on the stage.

'Rosie!' Just as she was feeling pretty pleased with herself, Rosie realised Ingrid had not shouted her name in a supportive way, in spite of the applause from the actors on stage, and Erin's grateful smile from the floor. Ingrid was standing with her hands on her hips just metres from the stage, her face beetroot red and that awful scarf flapping around her shoulders as she shook with rage.

'What *were* you thinking? Have you any idea how long it took us to put that beanstalk prop together? Bob's going to be working through the night now repairing that damage, and you could have killed poor Erin!'

Sod this, thought Rosie, but managed to keep the thought to herself. She simply nodded to Erin, and stalked from the stage. *This isn't a pantomime, this is the Nightmare Before Christmas.*

Ingrid's voice wafted behind her. 'Um, where are you going, Rosie?'

'Home,' said Rosie. 'This isn't worth my time. I've got presents to wrap.'

Rosie reached the fire exit that lead to the wardrobe shed where she'd left her bag, and pushed. The door ground open about an inch before a metallic scrape rang out. Puzzled, Rosie put her eye to the crack, and then turned to face the theatre.

'Why's this door chained shut?'

A few moments of panicked dashing about was enough to verify that all the doors had been secured with heavy chains from the outside. Confusion turned to anxiety: surely the hall's caretakers had noticed they were still rehearsing inside? Would someone be along at the end of the rehearsal to let them out?

'Hold on, our phones are all next door, how are we going to call anyone?'

Ingrid stood shivering with anger in the middle of the hall as the actors and crew checked and double checked each door, before finally exploding.

'*If* we could return to this *crucial* rehearsal, *please!*' Ingrid screamed, staring straight at the floor and spittle spraying from her mouth with every word. '*No one* will be needing to leave this hall for *at least* another two hours, and there will be plenty of time to open a door then.'

She finally looked up, to see the actors were now the ones staring at the floor, in embarrassment. She took a very visible deep breath and continued more quietly. 'Now. Starting positions. Act 1, Scene 4.'

Rosie found herself at the centre of an expanding circle of empty floor. She at least wanted to stare Ingrid down, but the director was already striding towards the lighting console. With an attempt at a haughty sniff, Rosie headed back to the wings, defeated.

The next few scenes and musical numbers were free of incident, but everyone was now on edge. Actors kept glancing at the doors they could see from the stage, and missing cues as a result. Rosie could *hear* Ingrid flouncing around the auditorium, and dreaded to think what effect that was likely to have on the cast. Thankfully, the petulant huffs and swishes of scarves died away after quarter of an hour or so, and the performances seemed to settle down.

By the time it came to the giant rat sequence, everyone was back in their stride, and the lighting crew were even laughing along with the gags; it was still only the second time that most of them had seen the show. The King, Queen, Dame and Simple Simon were getting ready to be chased off stage by scrawny Matt Harris in an unconvincing rat costume. It had been a leaden sequence in rehearsals, and they were just hoping the kids would respond to it on the night.

Rosie jumped as she heard a scrabbling sound at the door to the understage area where they kept the scenery flats between productions. How ironic, a real rat giving her the willies just as a fake one was about to make its entrance. She tried to ignore the noise, but then froze as she made out a faint groan underneath the scrabbling.

As quietly as she could, Rosie pulled the sturdy bolts on the double door and pulled it open.

Matt fell out, dressed in his rat costume apart from the head. He was in a bad way, and Rosie winced as she saw drying blood darkening his fair hair. She hauled the lad up the small step from the understage, and looked around for help. One of the male chorus was lurking by the props table and he dragged Matt back to the dressing rooms to make him comfortable.

What had happened? No one went under there during the show. Had he fallen through the trapdoor somehow? She'd have seen that, surely?

On stage, the Dame was cajoling the non-existent audience. 'Well, if you do see anything let us know, won't you, girls and boys?'

That was Matt's cue to start sneaking around behind the other actors; Ingrid would go absolutely crazy when he didn't show up on time. Rosie frowned. The outburst was already overdue, the actors looking confused at the lack of shouts from the technical crew and the lack of a student in a rat costume in their peripheral vision.

The trapdoor burst open and slammed back against the stage with a bang that echoed to the church hall's rafters. The actors all stayed in character and faced the front as the crew in the auditorium began to shout.

'Look out! Behind you!'

A monstrous shape had emerged from the trapdoor, blinking under the strong stage lights. Its face was thick with white greasepaint, with a lurid swathe of red across its lips and in large triangular patches on its cheeks, and tufts of brightly coloured hair flying off in every direction. This portly form was clad in a sparkling outfit that seemed to emphasise its size. Finally it stood upon the stage, six feet tall, and a long-bladed knife in each hand.

'*It's behind you!*' yelled everyone in the audience, as Rosie and the other backstage crew froze in horror. The actors still had their backs to the apparition and played along, pretending not to hear.

'Here we are again!' it screamed, and finally the Dame turned.

'Ingrid?' he said. 'You look ridiculous, what are you doing?'

He jumped back as Ingrid slashed at him with one of the knives, stumbling on the edge of the stage and almost tumbling into the orchestra pit.

'I make you laugh by night, but I am Grim-all-day!' she screeched. 'I am the Clown, and in Grimaldi's name I will prune this bastardised form of pantomime back to its dark roots in the Harlequinade and Commedia dell'Arte.'

The King, Queen and Simple Simon had all bolted for the steps down into the auditorium, but the Dame remained teetering on the lip of the stage. 'What's wrong with you, Ingrid?' he shouted in desperation. 'Dressing up as an 18th Century clown isn't going to sell out that matinée!'

'It's an anachronism for a time that never existed,' Ingrid raged, 'but tonight's tragedy will contain the seeds for a new comedic form, that celebrates the contribution of women to theatre!'

The Dame lowered his arms, shaking his head sadly. As Ingrid lunged towards him again, he stepped backwards into the orchestra pit, scrambling down over the piano to reach the floor.

'Tonight we amateur actors make history with blood, sweat and sacrifice!'

That does it! Rosie stepped out on to the stage. 'Ingrid, put those bloody knives down, you daft moose! Was it you who planted that firework? And nearly broke Erin's neck with that wire stunt?'

The Dame shouted up from the pit, as he eased his way round the drumkit to the auditorium. 'What are you talking about? She's been directing all night. We all heard her!'

Ingrid dropped one knife with a nasty grin, and pulled out a walkie talkie from her pocket. 'A little preparation, and a cheap radio. I sorted out your props table while I was at it, Rosie dear. It really wasn't that difficult,' she purred, 'but you've all been far too resourceful, so I have to be more direct.'

'Behind you!' crowed John from behind the lighting desk. Ingrid merely glowered at him through her garish makeup.

Then a black and white shape swiped the second knife from her grasp sending it wheeling into the pit where it narrowly missed the Dame.

Buttermilk the cow stood behind Ingrid, front hoof still raised in warning. 'If you try that again, you'll get an udder one,' it said in a broad West Country accent.

Ingrid spun round, and aimed what Rosie thought was probably supposed to be a kung-fu kick at Buttermilk, but whichever of the two Bobs was playing the front end blocked her easily, then turned to Rosie.

'What's going on?'

Rosie barely knew more than the rest of them, but she quickly filled the company in on the firework and Matt's injury. 'We'll have to call the police once we get our phones back,' she concluded.

To her surprise, the Dame shifted uneasily on his feet. 'Must we?' he asked. 'Apart from Matt, no one's actually hurt and... well, we open tomorrow. Can't we find a way to settle this internally? Everyone's worked so hard.'

Several other actors nodded slightly at this sentiment, though Buttermilk appeared unwavering. Surprisingly it was Ingrid herself who came to Rosie's defence.

'You could try and perpetuate these outmoded stereotypes as you'd planned, yes, but there is the small matter of the anthrax bomb I just planted under the stage.'

In spite of herself, Rosie dashed for the steps as quickly as she could, Ingrid not far behind her. 'It's just a few glass vials of anthrax, wrapped around a sherbet fountain stuffed with nails and black powder. You'd be amazed what the farmer's market can turn up if you know who to ask,' the lunatic continued.

'She must be lying,' whispered the Dame, his face pale beneath his make-up and moustache.

Rosie shook her head. 'Maybe, we have to check. Whatever it is, we need to get it out of the building.'

'Good luck,' trilled Ingrid, the gleam back in her eye. 'I'm pretty sure I felt one of the tubes break when I set it.'

Rosie folded her arms and arched an eyebrow. 'So we're trapped in a building with an unstable device about to blast anthrax over us, the understage area is contaminated, and we've no way of contacting the outside world?'

There was a pause as this summary sank in, and Rosie could feel the terror building. Being dreadful old hams, they'd probably clutch their brows and pretend to swoon rather than run around screaming, but once that panic started, she knew they were finished.

She was out of ideas. She was a retired art teacher and volunteer stage manager, not sodding Bruce Willis. She'd been roped into doing this bloody panto, and now she was going to face a lingering death at the whim of an unhinged director with unnervingly easy access to biological weapons. You just didn't get this nonsense with an evening of Alan Bennett monologues.

Even as Meryl started swaying on her pink-shoed feet, a modest cough from the stage made the whole company spin round. Buttermilk stood alone on centre stage, a determined poise to her fabric head, and her velour udders rippling with resolve.

'Cometh the hour... cometh the cow.' Buttermilk's body stretched as Bob F unfastened the catches between the two halves of the suit and took a step backwards into the open air.

He was still wearing his bulky respirator, but everyone could see his broad grin as he pointed to it in triumph, and he bowed as the cast applauded him.

———————

Five minutes later, Rosie and the braver actors gathered nervously in the wings by the door to the understage. There hadn't been a sound since Buttermilk had marched in, ducking her head under the low lintel and mooing as the door closed behind her. They'd all had a nervous laugh at the Bobs' adherence to the Method.

Ingrid was sitting on the stage now in the lotus position, wearing a serene smile at their efforts. Occasionally she'd shout things like 'you don't understand my vision,' but without any real rancour now.

'Are they all right in there?' asked Meryl with a frown. 'If they breathe some in, how long will they have?'

'I don't know,' snapped Rosie, 'If it's bacterial, well, they'll certainly have time to get out, won't they?'

'Will they?' asked Martin. 'Doesn't that mean they could contaminate us though?' The actors shifted a few feet further from the door.

'Embrace immortality, my mummers!' Ingrid was almost singing now, wreathed in smiles. 'This production will live in history as the birth of a new age of the Harlequinade!'

Rosie stood up with a shudder. 'We're missing something. Bob and Bob have walked into a trap.'

The Dame rubbed his moustache and adjusted his bosom. 'The old church's crypt ran underneath this hall. And below that, who knows? Take a few floor panels away... they could have broken their necks.'

Their last chance, poor Bobs, walking heroically to their doom in a cow suit. Of course there'd never been any anthrax, that was yet another trap. And if there was no bomb, how could they prove to the police that Ingrid had tried to murder them; that it was more than simply a tragic accident?

'It's just like the rocket, she's not tried to murder us herself, she's been pushing us into bumping ourselves off. She booby-trapped the understage.'

Rosie was interrupted as the door to the dressing rooms crashed open under a powerful kick from Buttermilk's leading hoof. 'She didn't, you know,' said the cow's rear end cheerfully.

Martin stepped forward amid the general noises of relief. 'Hang on, how did you get out? We've been waiting right by the door the whole time.'

'This one, yeah. We used the door on the other side of the stage. It's not much wider than a corridor down there and it's a pain in the bum turning round in this costume. Especially as... well, it might be harmless. But take a look.'

Buttermilk's mouth was clamped down on a bulky shape: clear tubes around a bright yellow cylinder, with two wires trailing from the top. The whole package was wrapped up with several layers of sellotape, but Rosie could still glimpse the words '*sherbet fountain*' in places.

'If it didn't go off when you broke the wire, I suppose we're safe,' said Rosie. 'We should try and get rid of it.'

'The wire was just to hang it,' trilled Ingrid, a thin line of drool leaking from her lips as she glanced across at her masterwork. 'I asked my son to knock up a watch battery timer inside. It should go off in, well, my watch hasn't got a battery, but pretty much nowish.'

There was no building tension this time, the actors leapt away from the deadly package in Buttermilk's mouth, shoving and scrambling over each other to get into the auditorium or the dressing rooms. Even the two Bobs panicked, and the bomb fell to the floor as the cow reversed back down the passageway as fast as she could.

Rosie dived forward faster than she would have thought possible, to catch the deadly sherbet fountain before it could shatter. She winced at the meaty smack as it slammed into her cupped bare hands. The bulky but surprisingly light package shifted, rolled, and threatened to slip from her grasp.

With a yell, Rosie pitched herself sideways. Her bad knee crashed against the floor, causing the bomb to jerk again from her grasp. She twisted on the floor, putting her whole body beneath her hands. Finally, she held it firm.

Looking around in vain for someone to help her to her feet, Rosie shifted the bomb from hand to hand as she pulled off her cardigan and bundled the device up in the woollen material. She was cradling an explosive device which was potentially stuffed with lethal bacteria. It could explode at any moment and fifty lives depended on her getting it out of a building that was chained shut.

She hauled herself back to her tired feet one-handed, grasping at the cold pipes of a radiator. She wasn't Bruce Willis, but she was Rosie Hadfield and for once in her life she knew exactly what she had to do.

As Rosie burst out of the wings on to the stage, Ingrid's face was unreadable beneath the thick greasepaint. She didn't even twitch at the sight of the bomb. She stared straight into Rosie's eyes. 'Rosie. I thought you *appreciated* theatre. Surely you can see what I was trying to do, to tear down this ridiculous reinforcement of patriarchal values that derides empowered women taking on cross-gendered identity constructs?'

Rosie hadn't wanted to give the woman the satisfaction of a reply, but couldn't help snorting as she strode downstage to the pyropots. She tied the bomb's trailing wire to the rocket, convincing herself the ticking noise she heard was a figment of her imagination.

'What are you doing?' asked Ingrid.

'You should be pleased,' said Rosie, reaching for the plug and ramming it into the pyropot. 'I'm spreading your message far and wide.'

'No!' Ingrid struggled to her feet as Rosie leaped from the stage and ran down the central aisle towards the lighting desk.

Ingrid lurched towards the pyropot...

Rosie skidded round the desk, grabbing the corner of the chunky black console to steady herself...

Ingrid reached forward to clutch at the wire...

A riot of coloured LEDs shone up at Rosie...

Ingrid gave a savage yell of triumph as she gripped the rocket...

Rosie pressed the button.

The rocket blasted from the stage with a thick cloud of smoke, and a deafening *whoosh!* Rosie whipped her head up as it punched straight through the ceiling, the bomb bobbing around beneath it for an uncertain instant.

She started to count under her breath even as she peered into the smoke to try and see what had become of Ingrid.

One elephant. Two elephant. Three—

BOOM!

In the sudden silence, the actors started to file on to the stage from the wings, a little sheepish. They kept as far away as they could from the smoking pyropot, where Rosie could just make out a huddled shape. She strolled down the aisle towards them, aware of shinsplints sending shooting jabs of pain up her leg with every step after her last exertion.

'Is it safe?' asked Bob F, stepping out of the cow suit at last, with his respirator dangling in one hand, leaving Bob G wearing a huge cow's head.

'I hope so. If it ever was really dangerous. If it was destroyed in the blast. Perhaps I've just started a shower of lethal rain over the home counties. I'm taking an umbrella home, that's for sure.'

'Look! The roof!' Phil was shouting, but not in panic, and the cast looked up and sighed at the fluffy white snowflakes that had started to drift down from the hole in the roof. 'Merry Christmas!'

They stood there for a long moment gazing up at the snow. The spell was broken by the sound of a siren in the distance, getting closer. Rosie looked down, to see a shape stirring by the pyropot. Ingrid looked badly burned, but everyone took a cautious step backwards nonetheless.

———

It was eight o'clock the next morning, and Rosie sat in her little VW Polo outside the church hall. She shivered in the sudden icy blast as Bob F opened the passenger door and climbed in, slamming the door with a clunk behind him and steaming up all the windows instantly.

'Well?' asked Rosie.

Bob shrugged, rubbing his bare hands together in a futile effort to warm them. 'About what we expected. They cancelled our booking thanks to the damage and we'll have to pay for the roof. They're pressing charges against Ingrid. Wouldn't want to be in her shoes when she comes round.'

Rosie took pity on him and nudged the Polo's heating up a notch. He held his hands in front of the fan with a grunt of gratitude. 'It could have been worse, Rosie. A lot worse.'

Rosie narrowed her eyes as she looked through the foggy window at the church hall entrance, the broken chains still lying where the fire crew had cut them.

She sighed. 'Yes, we had a lucky escape. Shame the roof's stuffed full of asbestos, really.'

Bob's hand flew to his mouth, but Rosie couldn't keep it up and a muffled snort soon became a giggle, which swelled to hysteria as the two friends sat in the tiny car and laughed until tears streamed down their cheeks.

'What are you doing for Christmas?' he asked when they'd finally regained some self-control.

Rosie's expression was determined as she turned the ignition with a savage twist, and pulled away from the kerb. 'What do you think, Bob? I'm planning next year's panto. The show must go on, dear.'

CONTRIBUTOR BIOGRAPHIES

THERESA DERWIN—THE EDITOR

Theresa was born and bred in Birmingham and her career has been pretty varied; from Warehouse Packer, then bar work, to being a crap waitress then swiftly into retail, Admin, Professional Student and dosser until finally entering the Civil Service in 1999. She left the Service in 2012 to pursue a career as a writer.

Theresa writes humorous fiction including SF, Urban Fantasy & Horror. She has twelve anthology acceptances behind her. She also writes a number of book reviews and at her site www.terror-tree.co.uk. Her short story collection *Monsters Anonymous* was released from Anarchy Books Sept 2012. She also produces feminist genre fanzine *Andromeda's Offspring*.

She has loved horror, fantasy and SF all her life, thanks to her father who raised her on 50s Sci-Fi Universal Monsters, tango and popcorn. Her love of the bizarre, (including her Dad) remains constant, to this day. She also owes a great debt to Rog Peyton from the BSFG who introduced her to alternative fiction at the tender the age of 14.

You can follow Theresa on Twitter @BarbarellaFem or find out more about her work at www.theresa-derwin.co.uk.

AUTHORS

Roger Clark lives in a Black Country town called Darlaston and thinks it is very much like Twin Peaks without the scenery. He was writing for local newspapers while at school and became a journalist when leaving education (but don't hold that against him as he never tapped a phone). He has written for a variety of publications such as the Radio Times, Doctor Who Magazine and DreamWatch (where he was listings editor). He wrote The Babylon 5 Security Manual with Jim Mortimore and Allen Adams and has also had his own radio show, presented on TV, acted, written plays, was a full time Press Officer and even found time to be active in fandom for quite a few years. His life is now pretty boring.

Based in London, Sean T Page manages the influential anti-ghoul website, ministryofzombies.com. His publishing credits include the Haynes Zombie Manual and the Official Zombie Handbook (UK) through Severed Press as well as numerous short stories. The undead trouble him greatly so follow the madness on his website and blog. He enjoys walks in the park and rain but not at the same time.

Colin Fisher lives in South East London with his cat Sammy, a short drive from the home of his loving wife Lisa (long story). His formative years were spent studying archaeology, listening to heavy metal, and arguing the finer points of Doctor Who continuity with an ever decreasing circle of friends. To his wife's exasperation, he remains deeply unfashionable to this day, a fact for which he neither apologises nor seeks approval. After an extended period of indolence in which he claimed to be 'managing' a bookshop, he now keeps body and soul together with something not dissimilar to IT in the City, although this is mainly a front for unspecified activities involving coffee, and snarling at people who approach him. His leisure hours—those that Southeast Rail sees fit to leave him with—are spent playing guitar, writing poetry and collecting and reading Tarot cards. When not shivering under a blanket in his half ruined pre-war garret or watching his cat's experiments in gene splicing with mice and frogs, he enjoys reading, and cites Tim Powers, Robert Holdstock and Kim Newman as his favourite myth makers.

He has two hugely talented children, and is inordinately proud of the fact that one also has a story appearing in this collection. He in no way accepts responsibility that a fascination with death, horror and psychopaths appears to run in the family, although early indoctrination with Dungeons & Dragons and violent video games seems to have paid off.

Colleen Chen is a Rolf Structural Integration practitioner and a writer residing in the Twin Cities after four years isolated in rural Brazil, where she wrote *Satan vs Santa* along with a novel and a number of other odd tales. She blogs at www. colleenchen.com and is a reviewer for the speculative fiction review site Tangent Online.

Caroline Cormack lives in London, UK, a city she loves. She has been writing fiction since childhood, although these days her stories feature more dead bodies and fewer ponies than they did back then. Her work has also been published in Bete Noire magazine.

Brandon Cracraft lives in the historic district of Tucson, Arizona with his boyfriend and a black cat. His stories have appeared in several anthologies including *The Touch of the Sea*, *Night Gypsy*, and *You Better Watch Out!* His first novel, *Family Values*, is available in both paperback and e-book format through Damnation Books. He is a member of the Horror Writers Association.

Edward Jeremy Marcus Beat didn't think he had a ghost of chance of getting a story published. Until he became one, that is.

Edward was in the first year of a Bachelor of Arts at the Wormsong University when he was shot by a couple of sky-thugs at a local internet café.

In the weeks following his death, he prevented the collapse of the internet and the end of civilisation as we know it.

Currently working as the spirit world's first official fairy godfather (following the landmark anti-discrimination case), Edward hopes to become famous with his self-help books for the recently undead.

Edward likes pizza, poltergeists, poetry and pointless alliteration.

Published Fiction: None—except for parts of his diary.

David Williamson has been writing horror for many years and was first published in the 28th Pan Book of Horror, followed by three tales in the 30th edition. Has has appeared in many other horror anthologies including 6 of the 10 Black Books of Horror series. He lives in West Sussex, enjoys hiking across the South Downs, likes real ale and playing blues guitar... very badly!

UZ Eliserio teaches popular culture at the Department of Filipino and Philippine Literature at the University of the Philippines, Diliman. His short stories can be found at uzeliserio.blogspot.com. For his works in Filipino, visit ueliserio.com.

Lucy Robertson lives in south-east England, and despite what her address would have you believe is closer to London than the countryside. Whereas other people look back with pride on their schooldays and droll yearbooks where they were voted 'most likely to succeed', 'most likely to become a millionaire', 'most likely to wake up in a gutter several counties away, missing trousers', etc, Lucy fondly remembers being nominated 'laziest', and has been striving to put minimum effort into meeting people's expectations ever since.

Lucy studied (in a loose sense of the term) 'Computer Science' at University, where she quickly stood out amongst her fellow students. Admittedly this may have been more due to being one of only eight girls in a class of ninety than because of a particularly notable work ethic on her part. Nevertheless, in her final year she blinded her tutors with an excess of curly brackets, semi-colons, and meaningless shorthand, and they were so impressed that no one noticed that none of her code actually worked.

A few months later she received a piece of paper telling her she had a degree, which she has since hidden away in case they realise their mistake and try and take it back.

When not writing or racking up a condemning list of Google searches in the name of 'research', Lucy enjoys gaming, digital art, reading graphic novels, reading things that aren't graphic novels, and watching high-quality films with friends. Ever in pursuit of that elusive quality that defines a masterpiece, they are fearful of the day they run out of things to watch on IMDB's 'Bottom 100' list, and there is some concern they may be forced to lower their standards.

Carl Lambein, Jr. resides in Northeast Ohio with his wife Deborah. He served as a Marine in Vietnam, and has worked as a teacher, car salesman, fishing guide, and real estate broker and developer. When not indulging in his favourite pastimes of reading and writing, he enjoys playing the banjo, fiddle, and guitar.

Fiona Moore is an anthropologist and writer based in Southwest London, and is currently a Reader at Royal Holloway, University of London. Her fiction and poetry has appeared in many venues, including Asimov's, Interzone, the British Fantasy Society Journal, and the Aurora Award-winning collection Blood and Water. Her non-fiction includes several guides to telefantasy series (most recently the two-volume By Your Command: The Unofficial and Unauthorised Guide to Battlestar Galactica). She has co-written three stage plays and four audio plays to date, and is the co-owner of audio production company Magic Bullet. Her website is www. fiona-moore.com. She actually quite likes Yoko Ono. best horror.

Spencer Carvalho has written short stories for various literary magazines and anthologies including the *Barcelona Review* and *Foliate Oak Literary Magazine*.

Andrew Lawston lives in London, where he publishes magazines. He has written more than 1,200 non-fiction articles on a freelance basis, but prefers writing fiction. His first published short story was All In A Day's Work, published in the Doctor Who charity anthology *The Cat That Walked Through Time* in 2001. Pierrot Le Who followed in 2008's *Shelf Life*.

Away from Doctor Who, he published original short stories in various small press publications and ezines between 2005 and 2010. Once all the rights reverted to him, Andrew self-published these stories in *Something Nice - Ten Stories* in 2012. Shortly afterwards his story A Lovely Cup of Tea was published in the anthology *A Splendid Salmagundi*.

A former French teacher, Andrew also holds an MPhil in Film Studies from the University of Birmingham, and self-published his thesis *Killing Me Softly? An Examination of the Depiction of Violence in the Early Films of Jean-Luc Godard* (1960-1967) in 2004 with Lulu, and on Kindle in 2013.

Andrew is currently finishing a translation of Giacomo Casanova's autobioraphical novel *Histoire de ma Fuite,* and his short story The Frag Prince will be published in the forthcoming *Grimm & Grimmer 4,* from Fringeworks.

In his spare time, Andrew acts in amateur dramatics productions for charity. Including more than a few pantomimes...

Thank you for taking the time to read this book, which we here at Fringeworks Ltd hope you enjoyed.

Feel free to find out more about our works at www.fringeworks.co.uk

You can follow the Editor Theresa Derwin on Twitter @BarbarellaFem

She writes book reviews at www.terror-tree.co.uk and her personal blog is www.theresa-derwin.co.uk

www.ingramcontent.com/pod-product-compliance
Lightning Source LLC
Chambersburg PA
CBHW050739230626
47052CB00003BA/534